PAPER BAG
REVOLVER

a novel by andy mascola

This novel is a work of fiction. Names, characters, places and incidents are either the product of the author's imagination or are used fictitiously. Any resemblance to actual events or locales or persons, living or dead is entirely coincidental.

For Brycen

There is no sun for me.

-Jay Reatard

THE CREW

My ride pulls into the lot just after ten in the morning. I pay the driver and step out of the cab and into the dusty mix of dirt and gravel where I'm scheduled to meet up with the crew. I take my duffel bag and suitcase from the car's backseat and shut the door, nodding to the driver. As I walk across the parking lot, I listen to the sound of earth and stone beneath the black rubber soles of my brown boots. The grinding crunch emboldens me.

Walt's motorcycle is parked between two old cars with FOR SALE signs in their windows. He's standing by the white van. His large, yellow backpack hangs from one shoulder. Inside Walt's luggage will be the detonators as well as his clothes, toiletries, and without a doubt his lucky bottle of whiskey that he brings on every job.

Walt leans back on the van, reaches into the inside pocket of his black sport coat, and takes out his cigarettes. He shakes one out and takes the filter between his lips, pulling it from the pack. With his other hand, he reaches into the front pocket of his tight black jeans and slides an orange lighter out. He squints as he lights the butt and takes a drag.

I drop my heavy duffel bag, which contains all my equipment, and reach around Walt for the handle on the van's side door. He steps out of the way as I slide it open, pushing first my suitcase and then my bag inside. Walt does the same with his backpack.

"You think Frank will let us smoke on the way?" I ask as I reach into the big pocket on the thigh of my cargo shorts and pull out a box of Marlboro reds and my lucky Zippo.

Walt shrugs. "I ain't betting he will. That's why I'm getting while the getting's good," he says, flicking the ash off the end of his cigarette before taking another drag.

"You two best get that shit out of your systems before you get in my van," Frank says as he walks around the vehicle from the opposite side and slides the side door shut.

I haven't seen Frank in three months, but he looks pretty much the same. Big, bald, old, wearing a white short-sleeve polo shirt one size too small, with thin, red horizontal stripes across the front and back. He looks at his watch and then reaches into the back pocket of his khaki slacks and pulls out a map.

"Jesus, Frank. You still ain't got GPS?" Walt asks before spitting in the dirt.

Frank ignores him as he opens the map and refolds it so that only the portion with a line drawn in red marker shows.

"I'll drive first," I say as I light my cigarette.

"No you won't," Frank says without looking up from the map. "Walt's driving first."

"Why?" I ask.

"Because I can't sleep while you're behind the wheel," Frank says.

"You mean you don't trust me," I say flatly.

"I mean, you drive like a fuckin' asshole is what I mean," Frank says, looking up at me. Walt laughs and a small cloud of smoke escapes from his mouth. Frank hands Walt the map and the key to the van, which is attached to a purple rabbit's foot keychain. "You guys eat?" Frank asks as he opens the passenger side door. Walt shakes his head.

"Just coffee," I say.

"We'll stop for chow on the way," Frank says, climbing into the passenger seat and shutting the door.

Walt flicks his butt into the dirt, walks around the van, and opens the driver side door. I enter first, stepping up into the van and sliding into the back between the two front seats.

"Where'd the bench go?" I ask, looking around.

"Took it out," Frank says.

"Why?" I ask.

"So you wouldn't have a place to sit," Frank says. Walt laughs as he shuts the driver side door and starts the engine. "I took it out so we'd have more room back there for equipment, why else would I take it out?"

"Where the fuck am I supposed to sit?"

"Better figure that out fast," Walt says as he puts the van into gear and steps on the accelerator.

I fall onto my bare knees on the thin carpet tacked to the floor of the van. "Son of a bitch!" I yell, rolling onto my ass while rubbing my knees. Walt continues to laugh as I pull my duffel bag

8

behind my head, find the softest place on it, and lie back while continuing to smoke the cigarette.

"Hey!" Frank yells from the front as he turns around in his seat.

"What?" I say as I exhale a stream of smoke through my nostrils.

"None of that shit in my van!" Frank barks.

Sighing, I sit up and open one of the small rear windows and push my cigarette out. Walt rolls down the driver side window and proceeds to light up.

"What about him?" I ask.

"Driver's privilege," Walt says, looking at me in the rearview. I hold up my middle finger. Walt grins maniacally.

"I'll have the number six," I say as I hand the waitress my menu.

"How do you want those eggs, honey?" she asks as she takes a pad out from the front of her apron and licks the end of a pencil before scribbling on the paper. Our waitress looks to be older than me, but not by much. Maybe she's in her early thirties. She's wearing lipstick and eyeliner, which makes it harder to tell. Her light brown hair is pulled up and back, a few stray, wavy strands hang down on either side of her face.

"Sunny side up," I say.

"What kind of toast?"

"White."

"And you?" she asks, turning to Walt who's sitting opposite me.

"I'll have the same, but make mine scrambled," he says, handing her his menu.

"And last but not least," she says, smiling at Frank who's sitting on the inside of the booth next to Walt.

"Give me the steak and cheese omelet with a side of home fries," he says, looking through a pair of spectacles perched on the tip of his nose. Frank hands the waitress his menu and takes off his glasses. He puts them inside a blue, plastic sleeve and slides it into the breast pocket of his polo.

"I'll put that order right in for you, boys," the waitress says as she turns and walks toward the kitchen.

Walt cocks his head to the side and bites his lower lip, watching our waitress as she walks away. "You can put something right in for me, baby, but it ain't my order," he says, winking at me and nodding. I wince and stir my coffee. "She's got some heft. I like a woman with heft," Walt says.

"Heft?" I ask.

"You know, she's got a bit of meat on her. I like that. You can tell she's had a kid or two. Her tits are kind of saggy and they sway a bit. You can tell those legs have held up some weight. She's spent some time on that ass. She's got that secretary spread going on," Walt says.

"Secretary spread?" I ask, taking a sip of coffee.

"Don't you know nothin' of the world, Jesse?" Walt says, putting both hands on the table and leaning toward me. "Secretary spread," he says again slowly. I shrug. "Jesse, what do secretary's do all day?" Walt asks, shaking his head in disbelief.

"I don't know, answer phones?"

Frank chuckles into his coffee.

Walt runs his hand through his black, spiky hair. "Do you believe this kid?" he says to Frank. Frank shakes his head. "They sit, Jesse," Walt says. "Secretaries sit! When ladies sit for too long, all day every day, their asses spread. Hence the term secretary spread."

"Gotcha," I say, taking a sip of the coffee.

An older waitress walks over with a pot of freshly brewed coffee. "Can I warm those mugs up for you, fellas?" she asks.

"Please," Walt answers, holding his mug out to be filled. "Pardon me…Carla?" Walt says, staring at the waitress' nametag. "If I asked you what secretary spread is, what would you tell me?"

"I'd say that's when your caboose gets wide from sitting on it all day," Carla says. "You?" she asks, motioning with the pot to Frank. He puts his hand over the top of his mug and shakes his head. Walt holds up his mug as if toasting me and smiles his toothy grin as if to say 'see?' I nod and shrug.

I'm standing outside the van, smoking a cigarette when Walt and Frank exit the diner. Walt walks past me and unlocks the driver side door before tossing the van key over his shoulder.

"Your turn, Jesse," he says as I just miss the key, trying to grab it from the air with one hand. Walt climbs into the van and slides between the front seats and into the back.

I pick up the key, climb into the driver's seat, and shut the door. I unlock the passenger side for Frank, roll down my window, and pick the map up out of the center console. Frank gets in and shuts the door.

"How much farther would you say, Frank?" Walt asks from the back of the van.

Frank looks at his watch. "I'd say we'll be there around lunch time."

"What kind of job is this?" I ask.

"Car dealership," Frank says.

"What kind of car dealership keeps a safe full of cash inside?" Walt asks.

"The kind of car dealership that used to be a bank," Frank says.

"How do you know there's anything in it?" I ask.

"Inside man," Frank says. "Son-in-law of the old man who owns the place. Says he's looking to disappear. Had all the details except the combination."

"What's in it for him?" I ask.

"Twenty-five percent," Frank says.

"Twenty-five percent?" Walt says incredulously. "Hell, you're only giving me and Jesse ten apiece!"

"Yeah? And what's ten percent of nothing, smart guy?" Frank asks.

Walt sighs and falls back on my duffel bag. "This is some bullshit," he says.

I start the engine and pull out of the diner's parking lot. As I drive, I think back on the last time I saw my older brother alive. He was playing pinball in the snack bar of a bowling alley.

11

THE PAST

"Hey," I say as I step up to the side of the machine. I watch the silver ball bouncing around the mushroom-shaped bumpers under the glass. "You wanted to see me?"

"Yeah, hang on, Jesse," my brother says. "Hey, kid, you want to take over here?" Bill steps away from the pinball machine, and a teenage boy slides in and takes over the game. "Follow me," he says. I follow him through the bowling alley and out into the parking lot. He unlocks his black Charger and we both get in. I take out a cigarette and my Zippo. "What do you think you're doing?" Bill asks.

"Smoking?"

"Not in my car," he says as he reaches into his shirt pocket, pulls out a small vial, and unscrews the black plastic cap. He taps out a bump of coke onto the knuckle of his thumb and snorts it. "You want a hit?" he asks as he screws the cap back on the tiny glass jar.

"No," I say as I push my unlit cigarette back into the pack.

"You know that guy I told you about?" Bill asks as he puts the vial of cocaine back into the pocket of his jeans.

"What guy?"

"That guy Frank," Bill says as he pinches his nostrils and looks in the rearview mirror.

"The guy who's been putting a crew together?"

"Well, you and I would call it a crew, but he's actually just taking me and one other dude."

"How many guys does it take to make up a crew?" I ask.

"How the fuck should I know, Jesse? Listen, that's not the point. The point is, he wants me on his next job."

"That's great! This is what you wanted, right?"

Bill nods, takes the vial out of his pocket again, and taps out some more coke onto his knuckle before snorting it.

"How much does it pay?" I ask.

"This first job? If there's as much in this safe as Frank seems to think there is...," Bill drums on his thighs. "I should be walking out with at least ten grand."

"Holy shit," I say. "That'll be great for you and Samantha and the baby."

"I can get us out of the dump we're in now, that's for sure," Bill says as he turns and looks out of the driver side window while rubbing his nose with the palm of his hand. "How about you?" he asks, turning toward me. "You been practicing?"

"With the drill you gave me?"

"With everything."

"Yeah, I mean, I've made more holes in the dumpster behind Sal's than I can count. I heard Sal bitching about it to the trash guy who brings the truck around every week to empty it."

Bill laughs. "What'd the guy say about the holes?"

"He was just, like, shrugging and saying, 'I don't know what to tell you, Sal. Those holes weren't there when I dropped it off. This is the third dumpster I've brought you guys in the last two months!'"

Bill laughs super hard at my impression of the dumpster delivery guy. "You want to get some *real* practice?"

"Yeah, you know I want to get some real practice."

"No, I mean, like, tonight."

"Tonight?"

Bill nods.

"Shit yeah!" I say. "But I don't have my equipment with me."

"You can use my gear. It's in the trunk."

Real practice meant going to the public transit depot and breaking into parked buses, train cars, and utility trucks. There was nothing of value to take, it was more like school. Bill would show me how to use the tools of the trade. And while it wasn't the same as safecracking, it gave me experience with the equipment and the different key entry locks, bolts, and combination types. Bill would bring everything from heavy duty bolt cutters, hydraulic drills and bits, right on down to picks and tiny wrenches that you could stash in a wallet. He was an expert with all this stuff, and he took time to show me how to use it.

Little did I know then, but that night would be the last time I'd see my big brother alive. He called me all excited right after he'd finished the job. It had paid off twice as much as he'd hoped. Within a week, he and Samantha and the baby moved out of the rented single bedroom apartment they were living in and put a down payment on a condo upstate. He wanted me and mom to come up and visit after he returned from his next job…his last.

Our mom had no idea what my brother Bill did. She assumed he was a well-paid locksmith. I'll never forget the day we got the call about the accident. I heard our mother wailing over the sound of Iron Maiden blaring through my headphones. I jumped out of bed, ripped the cans from my ears, and ran into the kitchen. Mom was sitting at the kitchen table with her face in her hands.

"He's dead, Jesse!" she yelled.

"Who's dead, mom?" I asked, not remembering my brother was traveling back that day.

"Bill's dead," she whispered.

"What?"

I ran out the front door and threw up on the lawn. It was a warm, sunny day and not at all reflective of the horror that we'd just experienced upon learning of my brother's demise.

My mother walked outside, knelt beside me in the grass, and began rubbing my lower back. "It was a car accident," she said.

That night, mom and I drove up north to visit Samantha and the baby at the new condo. The mother of my brother's child answered the door in tears. Bill's daughter, Jolene, was over Samantha's shoulder as she softly bounced her. My brother's girlfriend didn't say anything as she turned and walked into the living room and sat down on the new couch. Mom and I followed her.

"The cops said the Charger's driver side tire blew. He skidded off the highway and hit a tree head-on. The airbag never opened. He wasn't wearing a seatbelt. His head went through the windshield. They pronounced him dead when the EMTs showed up. They dropped off his stuff an hour ago," Samantha said, as she motioned to the duffel bag by the sliding glass door that led out to the deck.

"Would it be okay if I take a look?" I asked as I moved toward my brother's equipment bag.

"Go ahead," Samantha said. I unzipped the bag and looked over Bill's tools without taking them out. They were all there. I zipped the duffel back up and stood with my hands on my hips. "Take them with you when you leave, Jesse," she said. I turned around to look at her. "He would've wanted you to have them."

Mom and I left with Bill's black duffel bag in the trunk of her car. I smoked a cigarette and stared out the passenger side window at the blur of buildings and trees as we drove back home.

It wouldn't be until the day of the funeral that I'd meet Frank for the first time. I was wearing a black button-down shirt and tie with black jeans. I didn't own dress pants.

It was a cold, cloudy, sunless day. Mom was a wreck. Fortunately, her two older brothers were there to keep her company and listen to her stories about when Bill was younger.

After the coffin was lowered into the ground, I moved away from the funeral and lit a cigarette, walking along the street. I unbuttoned my sleeves and rolled them up just below my elbows. Behind me I heard a car. I turned. The tinted driver side window of a black Cadillac slowly slid down.

"You must be the brother," the man inside said. "Bill talked about you." The guy was old and bald but otherwise healthy looking, with a kind smile. He shut the car's engine off and opened the door. He wore a black suit and tie over a white button-down shirt. He stood only slightly taller than myself, jiggling some change or keys in his pants' pockets. "What's your name, kid?" he asked as he lifted his sunglasses and rested them on his bald head. He had friendly eyes that made me trust him right away.

"Jesse," I said.

"My name's Frank. Your brother worked for me." He stuck out his right hand. I put the cigarette between my lips, freeing my right hand, and shook the old man's cool pillowy paw. "Bill said you were good with tools. Would you say you're as good with tools as your brother was?" Frank asked.

"I'm okay," I said, as I shrugged and blew a stream of smoke from the side of my mouth.

"You got any equipment of your own?"

I nodded. "I got all my brother's stuff."

Frank's face lit up. He reached into the inner pocket of his sport coat and pulled out a thick brown envelope. "Give this to your

15

mother," he said, holding the envelope out to me. I took it and stuffed it into the back pocket of my jeans. He reached into the opposite inside pocket and pulled out a small white card. I took it from him and looked at it. No name, no address, not even a website, just a phone number printed in black. "Take care of your mother and your brother's family. When that envelope's empty, call the number on that card, and I'll put you to work for me."

Frank replaced the sunglasses over his eyes and sat back down behind the wheel. He started the car, and the black tinted window slid all the way up so I could no longer see him. I pushed the card into my front chest pocket and watched as the big automobile drove out of the cemetery and down the street.

LUNCH

"Get off at the next exit," Frank commands as he looks at the map through the same spectacles he'd been wearing in the diner.

I look in the rearview mirror as I put the blinker on and shoot a glance back at Walt. He's asleep on his side, his head on my duffel bag, his hands sandwiched between his knees. I get off at the next exit. At the end of the ramp is a blue sign with a white knife and fork and an arrow pointing right.

"Follow your nose, kid," Frank says.

I put the right turn signal on and pull into a Denny's parking lot. I park the van and kill the engine. Walt wakes and yawns.

"Where are we?" he says groggily.

"Denny's," I say.

Frank gets out of the passenger seat.

"Do me a favor, Jesse," Walt says as he stretches. "Open this side door so I don't have to climb through the front."

I sigh, jump out the driver side door, walk around to the other side of the van, and slide the door open. I light a cigarette and turn to see Frank walking into the restaurant ahead of me and Walt.

"Give me a light, would ya?" Walt asks, shaking out a butt. I hand him my closed Zippo. Walt's shoulders drop tiredly, and he gives me a look as if to say, 'You can't even be bothered to light it for me?' He lights his cigarette and hands me back the Zippo. "Shit!" he says, leaning back with his hands on his lower back. "This van ain't meant for sleeping, that's for damn sure!" I walk over to where the front of the van meets the sidewalk and sit on the curb. "You reckon this is the town where the job is?" Walt asks. I shrug. "How long I been sleeping?"

"I've been driving for just about two hours," I say.

"Did we stop for gas?"

"Mmm mmm," I say, shaking my head.

"I had the most fucked up dream," Walt says. "I dreamt I was walking around inside a giant department store, carrying a toilet seat, trying to find someone who could give me a price on it. Anyway, I'm walking past a lady mannequin in the sportswear department, and out of the corner of my eye, I swear I see it move. So, I stop and turn to look at it, and sure enough, it's looking at me."

"Did it have eyes?" I ask.

"Huh?"

"Most mannequins don't have eyes. How did you know it was looking at you?"

"This mannequin didn't have eyes either. It had one of them creepy, smooth faces with no holes. I only knew it was looking at me because its head was turned in my direction."

"Then what happened?" I ask, taking a drag off my cigarette.

"Then I slowly turned and continued walking, and I'm just about out of the sports department when I hear something. So, I figure it's finally someone who can help me get a price on the damn toilet seat, you know?"

I start laughing. Walt smiles.

"I turn a corner and there's what looks like a male mannequin standing in the aisle, wearing camouflage and holding a crossbow pointed directly at me! The mannequin pulls the trigger, I spin just as the arrow whizzes by, and I see it land in a column next to me at head level! I turn to run but standing not fifteen feet away is the woman mannequin from the sportswear department. So, I hurl the toilet seat at her like a Frisbee. It hits her square in the tits and she falls backward all stiff-like.

"At this point, I gotta get out of there, you know? So, she's on the ground, and as I run by, she grabs my ankle. I kick my foot forward as hard as I can and her entire arm comes off her body. Now I'm running toward the exit, dragging this mannequin arm, but as soon as I get to the glass doors, they're all locked! I start pushing and pulling on them as hard as I can, but they don't budge. Behind me, I hear footsteps. I turn and see every mannequin in the department store coming at me. They surround me as I continue to struggle with the doors. And just when they're about to touch me, that's when I wake up."

"Wow, that's a fucked up dream, man," I say.

"I ain't had a dream that fucked up in a long time," Walt says, laughing.

I take a final drag off my butt before dropping it onto the pavement and crushing it with my boot as I stand.

Walt flicks his cigarette into the nearby woods and follows me into the restaurant. Frank is sitting on a small bench built into the wall. He stands as the hostess comes out from behind her desk and takes three menus off a podium.

"Follow me, please," she says. Walt and I follow Frank and the hostess to a booth in the back corner of the Denny's. "Can I start you off with something to drink?" she asks.

"Coffee," Walt says.

"Same," I say.

"You got V8?" Frank asks.

"The vegetable kind? Yeah, we've got that," the hostess says. "Your waitress will be right out with your drinks."

Walt takes a good look at the hostess as she's walking away from our table.

"Enough heft on that one for you?" I ask.

"Not nearly enough."

After lunch, we check into a motel down the street from the Denny's. Frank's booked us separate rooms in advance, all side by side, with doors that exit into the hall. As I piss, I can hear Walt next door, laughing at something on TV.

Frank discourages us from going out too much during the day. The concern is that if too many people see us, we'd be easier to describe. I change into a pair of gym shorts I brought to sleep in and step out onto the deck that overlooks the parking lot. My room is between Frank's and Walt's. I'm just about to light up a cigarette when I hear Frank's voice coming from his room's sliding door.

"Hello, Jack, it's Frank. How's she doing?" I can only hear one side of the conversation, but from what I can gather, Frank's talking to someone he's close with. "Jesus Christ," I hear him say before he sighs heavily. "What can I do to help?" there's a pause. I hear what sounds like a pencil on paper. "How much longer does the doctor say she has?" Another pause. "Right. Okay. I should be back before then." I hear a chair being pushed back and see Frank step out of his room onto the deck. I slowly step backward into my room and continued to listen. "I know you are, Jack. None of that matters now. You're my brother-in-law, and regardless of the disagreements we've had in the past, you've always been good to Caroline." Another pause. "I know you will, Jack. I appreciate what you're doing. I know it can't be easy with the kids all grown up and dealing with problems of their own. I'll give you a call when I get back to the city. I've got the list. I'll do my best to get these things before I see you again. Okay…give her my love, will ya?"

I watch through the white, plastic, vertical blinds as Frank shuts his phone off and slides it into his pants pocket before going back into the room. The door to the deck slides shut. I lean against the wall and hear what sounds like muffled crying coming from Frank's room. I step outside, lean back against the railing, and light a cigarette.

I take the complimentary pool towel off the rack in the bathroom and walk downstairs in my trunks. An older man is swimming laps. In the corner is a hot tub. I put my towel on a chair and walk over to a timer on the wall, turning the dial for the maximum allowed running time of forty minutes. I gently lower myself into the hot, bubbling water, submerging myself completely. Upon standing, I push my hair back on my head. I need a haircut. I sit on the bench built into the side of the tub, positioning my lower back in front of one of the tub's jets while I watch the old man swim laps. I tilt my head back and close my eyes, thinking about Frank's phone call. I never imagined him to have any family, let alone a sick sister.

When I open my eyes and lift my head, there's a woman sitting across from me. She's gently patting the hot water from the tub onto her face with her hands, being careful not to get her brown, wavy hair wet. She's pretty, with dark, round, sleepy eyes that remind me of Mila Kunis.

"Water's nice," I say.

"What?" she says, looking at me for the first time.

"The water."

"Oh, yeah, this is how I've ended every day since I've been here," she says.

A young man and woman walk into the pool area and put their things down on a table nearby. The old man has disappeared.

"Business?" I ask.

"Huh?"

"Are you here on business?"

20

"Oh…yeah. I don't like being away from home, but I will miss this tub when I'm gone. You here for work, too?"

"Yeah," I say.

The young couple get into the tub. I slide down the bench, closer to the woman with the Mila Kunis eyes, to make room for the couple.

"How are ya?" the guy asks me, nodding.

I smile and nod back.

"I'm not going to stay in too long," the young woman says to the man.

"We just got here," he says, sounding slightly annoyed.

"I told you when we left the restaurant I wasn't feeling well," she says. The man sighs and shakes his head. "I'll just go back to the room," she says and starts to stand.

"Are you kidding?" he asks.

I look over at Mila Kunis Eyes, and she's looking down, pretending not to be listening. I lean my head back.

"Kim," I hear the young guy say. The young woman exits the tub. The guy turns around on the bench, watching the woman dry herself at the table where they'd put their things. "Kim," he says again, louder this time. The woman grabs her things off the table, slips on her flip-flops, and exits the pool area.

The young guy turns back and rests his elbows on either side of himself on the edge of the tub. He shakes his head and sighs. After less than a minute, he clears his throat and exits the jacuzzi. He grabs his towel and things from the table and leaves.

"He forgot his flip-flops," I say.

The woman with the Mila Kunis eyes laughs. "That was awkward," she says.

"Definitely," I say. "What do you do?"

"I manage a Maxine's."

"A what?"

"Maxine's?"

"I don't know what that is."

"It's a clothing store that sells women's apparel. It's a fairly new chain."

"Oh! Okay, well, then, that would explain why I've never heard of it."

21

"I'm in town for training. What about you?"

"I'm a locksmith," I say.

"Do you love it?"

"I'd never thought about it, but yeah, I guess I do love it," I say. "What about you? Do you love what you do?"

"I love fashion, but spending every day in retail isn't exactly my dream."

"What is your dream?"

"I'd eventually like to be a designer."

"Women's clothing specifically?"

"Women's and men's." After a pause, she says, "Hey, are you good with car locks?"

"Yeah, sure. Why?"

"I've got this rental they gave me at the airport. The passenger side door won't open from the outside. If you have a moment, do you think maybe you can take a look?"

"Sure," I say, shrugging.

"The weird thing is, it worked fine at the airport. Like, I definitely remember opening the passenger side door and putting my stuff on the seat. Ever since then, it hasn't worked. I mean, I can open it from the inside, but not the outside."

"Did you touch anything on the inside of the door? Like, when you open the door, where the lock mechanism is. Did you flip something in there at all?" I ask.

"I don't think so. If I did, it wasn't intentional."

"I can't promise anything, but I don't mind taking a look at it for you."

"Are you sure?"

"Yeah."

"You want to check it out right now?"

"Why not?" I say.

I let her get out of the hot tub first. She's wearing a blue and white bathing suit. It's obvious she knows clothing as the bathing suit fits her perfectly and isn't too modest nor too revealing. I notice a brown, round birthmark about the size of a nickel on the back of her knee. Her legs are shaved and they appear toned. I think about Walt's comment about women with heft. I wouldn't say this woman

22

has heft. Her body seems well proportioned, and she doesn't appear to be carrying any extra weight.

I follow her out of the tub to a nearby table where her things are. I take my towel from the chair and dry myself off. We try not to look at one another. She wraps a towel around her waist and picks up her keys and phone. I throw the towel around my shoulders and nod.

She turns and walks out of the pool area. I follow her through the motel lobby, out the front doors, and into the parking lot. She's wearing brown flip-flops that create a soft, slapping rhythm as she crosses the pavement to a dark blue Nissan sedan parked in the shade of a tree.

"Okay, watch this," she says. She double clicks the button on her key. The car's headlights blink and the doors unlock themselves. She opens the driver side without a problem. "Try the passenger side," she says.

I try the passenger side handle and nothing happens. I try the back door on the same side of the car and it opens.

"See?" she says.

"Hmmm," I say, rubbing my chin.

"Now watch," she says. She ducks into the driver side of the car and opens the passenger side door from the inside, pushing it toward me. I take the handle and pull it open all the way, and my eyes are suddenly looking directly down the front of her bathing suit. I quickly look up at her face. She backs out of the driver side. I clear my throat and begin to examine the inside of the door where it meets the body of the car. She comes around to my side and looks over my shoulder as I squat down and examine the inside of the door area. "What do you think it is?" she asks.

"Do you have a screwdriver?"

She steps around me and sits in the passenger seat. She opens the glove compartment and looks under the manual. "There's a pen," she says hopefully.

"That may work," I say, taking it from her. I use the back end of the pen to shift a slightly obscured switch in the inside part of the door from right to left. "Let's give it a try now," I say. I step back as she gets out of the car and shuts the passenger side door, then attempts to open it. It doesn't budge.

"Nope," she says.

"Try hitting the button again," I suggest. She hits the button on the key twice. The car beeps and the lights flash. She hits the button two more times. The lights flash again and we hear the locks release. "You want to do the honors?" I ask. She pulls the handle, and the passenger side door opens.

"You did it!" she says. "Thank you so much."

"It's what I do," I say. "Any idea what time it is?"

She looks at her phone, "It's coming up on three o'clock."

"You want to get a coffee?" I ask.

"Sure, but it's on me."

"I should probably put some clothes on," I say.

"Same. Meet me in the lobby in twenty minutes?"

"I'll see you there," I say.

I jog across the parking lot toward the door to the motel's entrance.

"Hey!" she yells from where she's still standing next to the open passenger door of her rented Nissan. I stop and turn. "What's your name?"

"Jesse! What's yours?"

"Dawn!" she says.

"I'll see you in the lobby in twenty minutes," I say, turning and jogging into the motel.

I take a quick shower and change into jeans, a green t-shirt, and my boots. When I get to the lobby, I see Dawn sitting in a chair, looking at her phone. She's wearing white shorts, a green and white striped short-sleeve shirt, and her flip-flops.

"Hey," I say as I approach.

"Hey," she says, standing up and sliding her phone into the back pocket of her shorts.

I follow her outside. We stand together on the edge of the parking lot, waiting to cross. We're both looking up and down the street. Cars pass from both directions. Something makes me turn and look back at the motel, and that's when I see Frank, standing on his deck with a drink in his hand. I wave. He doesn't wave back. He's wearing aviator sunglasses, and although I can't tell where he's looking, he's clearly watching us.

"Who are you waving at?" she asks.

"Huh? Oh, just some guy standing on his deck," I say.

"Well aren't you friendly!" she says, laughing while looking back and forth, waiting for a break in the traffic. I shrug and smile. "I think this is the best it's gonna get," she says as she slowly begins to walk across the street. I follow, and after a car passes going in the opposite direction, we both run across.

We step inside a small coffee shop called Rise and Grind. It has white walls and a checkerboard tiled floor. There are two small tables in the corners on either side of the door, each with two cheap-looking wooden chairs, and a small cream and sugar station with napkins and stirrers near the front counter. None of the décor inside the coffee shop intones what's being sold here. There's barely anything to the place. It doesn't even smell like a coffee shop. It might as well be a DMV. In the very back of the establishment, behind the barista, is a short menu written in different colored chalk on a small blackboard.

At the counter is a young, bored-looking girl in glasses, wearing a black apron over a white t-shirt. Dawn and I are the only customers.

"Is this your first time here?" I ask.

"Third," she says. "The coffee's way better here than it is at the continental breakfast in our motel's lobby. What looks good to you?"

"I'm going to follow your lead," I say.

Dawn steps up to the counter. "I'll have a medium Iced Durango with cream and sugar," she says before motioning to me.

"I'll have the same, but without sugar and just a small amount of cream."

Dawn pays for the drinks. We get straws and napkins, and I follow her to one of the small tables by the door. I take a sip of the Durango. It tastes like a mix of caramel and vanilla.

"Not bad," I say.

"So…," she says.

"So…," I say. "You married?"

I've caught her with this question mid-sip. She coughs, covering her mouth with a napkin. "Am I married?" she asks from behind the napkin.

"Too personal?"

"No."

"No, as in not too personal, or no as in you're not married?"

"Both. No, as in it's not too personal a question, and no, I'm not married. What about you?" she asks.

"Nope. Boyfriend?" I ask.

"Nope," she says. "Unless you count Jasper."

"Cat?" I ask.

"Yep. Girlfriend?"

"No," I say, and then I lean forward, cross my eyes, and loudly slurp the Durango directly from the edge of the cup without picking it up from the table. She laughs.

"What do you think that couple in the hot tub are doing right now?" Dawn asks.

"I'm guessing things are either going really well or really terribly...or maybe she just needed to use the bathroom."

"Maybe she wanted sex," Dawn says.

I'm caught mid-sip and begin coughing. "Maybe," I manage to say as I hold a napkin in front of my mouth.

After we have our coffees, Dawn and I walk back across the street to the motel. She tells me she's got to get ready to have dinner with the people in her training class. I reach out my hand to shake hers. She laughs and gives me a hug.

"Give me your phone," she says.

"I don't have one."

"You don't have a phone?"

"No," I say, shrugging.

Dawn walks over to the front desk. I watch as she writes something on one of the business cards. She comes back and hands it to me. On the card is her name and phone number.

"Call me," she says.

"You mean, like, when I get back home?"

"Sure," she says.

"Okay, thanks," I say, pushing the card into my back pocket.

Back in my room, I kick off my sneakers, lie on the bed, and turn on the TV. I'm watching a tabloid news show about Ashton Kutcher's new girlfriend. On the screen are images of the actor and his new "gal pal" having lunch outside and walking on the beach. I slide the business card out of my back pocket and look at Dawn's name and number.

Someone knocks on the door to my room. I look through the eyehole and see Frank standing outside. I open the door.

"How was the coffee?" he asks.

"The coffee? Oh, yeah, it wasn't too bad."

Frank doesn't say anything; he just stares at me. After a moment, he clears his throat, and I realize he's waiting for me to explain myself.

"I know you don't like us leaving the motel or talking to anyone while we're on a job, Frank. That woman I was with is from out of town, so I figured..."

"I don't ask much of my crew," Frank says, interrupting me. "But the one thing that could get us all pinched is a decent description to law enforcement by anyone we come into contact with before we beat feet out of town. I expect you and knucklehead to use your best judgement when interacting with anyone, even if it's just a clerk selling you a pack of gum."

"Got it," I say, nodding and looking down.

"Have you eaten?" he asks.

"Not yet," I say.

"Don't bother. Get your gear together and meet me at the van in a half hour. We'll hit a drive-thru on the way to the job."

THE JOB

I'm standing outside the van, smoking a cigarette, holding the duffel bag with my equipment in it. I'm wearing the same clothes I wore for my coffee with Dawn. Walt walks into the parking lot with Frank. Neither of them look happy.

"I'm driving," I say as I watch Walt unlock and slide the van's side door open.

"I'm driving," he says.

"You're both wrong," Frank says, taking the keys out of Walt's hand. "I'm driving."

Frank pays for burgers, fries, and sodas in a drive-thru at a tiny local chain called Sweet Boys' Burgers. We eat on the road. It's not the best burger and fries I've ever had, but it certainly isn't the worst. By the time we're on the highway, heading to the job, it's beginning to get dark.

Frank turns the van radio to an oldies station. The Bo Diddley song Who Do You Love? is playing. I'm listening to the lyrics and trying to imagine a chimney made out of a single human skull. I picture a skinny pipe-like chimney that doubles as a neck, with a skull at the top that has smoke pouring out of its eyes, nose, and mouth. Walt has been remarkably quiet since we ate.

After a fifty-minute drive, Frank pulls into the parking lot of a dealership. It's dark, but there's a single shining light on a pole. The cars are a mix of Hondas, Volkswagens, and Toyotas. Nothing American. Frank drives the van through the rows of vehicles and around to the back of the single-story office building where there's a rear door with a sign that says Employees Only.

He parks the van near the edge of the woods. We all grab our respective gear. Frank hands each of us a pair of black leather gloves before he fastens a wide leather carpenter's belt around his waist that holds a large flashlight as well as two empty canvas sacks, which hang off his hips like holsters. Walt steps out of the van and pulls his yellow backpack over his shoulders.

I exit through the van's side door and follow Walt and Frank to the Employees Only entrance. I watch as Frank holds the flashlight for Walt who takes the backpack off and begins to rig the

28

door with plastic explosives. Fortunately, the nearest thing to us is a gas station that, judging by the grass growing through the cracks in the pavement and the price per gallon, appears to have closed years ago.

Walt maintains a serious demeanor while working. I can't imagine Frank would have him on the job if he didn't. Frank holds the long flashlight steady as Walt rigs the door lock to blow. He works fast, and after about three and a half minutes, he nods and says, "Okay."

Frank shuts the flashlight off, and the three of us duck behind a dumpster. Walt hits a button on a box the size of a walkie-talkie. The lock on the door sizzles and smoke can be seen in the moonlight followed by a flash and a loud pop. The door opens slightly outward. The three of us hustle inside.

No sooner do we enter than we hear the high-pitched sound of an alarm system in its preliminary stage of alert. Frank reaches into a pouch on his belt, pulls out a small notecard, and hands it to Walt. Again, Frank holds the flashlight over his shoulder as Walt alternately looks down at the code on the card and then at the illuminated keypad, punching the numbers from the card into the alarm system.

The high-pitched tone stops and Walt turns toward Frank. "Where to?" he asks.

We follow Frank to an office door and find it unlocked. I flick on the light switch, illuminating the room.

"Shut that light off!" Frank shouts.

I immediately turn it off. "Why?" I ask.

"This dealership may be in the middle of nowhere, but even nowhere is somewhere. You can see that light from outside. Anyone passing by on the main road may get suspicious," he says. "We have to move fast. The owner of this place may be notified any time someone enters the premises afterhours."

Walt and I watch as Frank walks over to a wall and removes a conspicuous-looking painting of a sailboat housed in a thick gold frame. Behind the painting, a safe built into the wall is revealed. It looks to be at least fifty years old. I imagine a more experienced safecracker would be able to open it with a trained ear and a stethoscope, but I'm not experienced with the inner workings of a safe of this age. I work with a drill and rely on good old fashioned TNT.

I put my bag down and unzip it. With Frank's flashlight over my shoulder, I first find the headlamp I wear that allows me to work in the dark. I pull it over my hair and switch it on. From my bag, I take out a rubber mallet and a metal stake. I put the stethoscope on and set to work tapping around the lock, listening to the reverberations. As soon as I've isolated the hollow areas around the dial, I can begin drilling.

Frank and Walt go from office to office, looking through drawers and cabinets, taking any loose cash that may be lying around.

As I begin to isolate hollow points around the lock, I mark each one with a small X using a piece of orange chalk. After I've made three Xs on the door to the safe, I take the drill out from my duffel bag as well as my box of bits. I carefully hold up each one to the Xs to make sure I'm not going to make a hole that's too big. I don't want to risk Walt's explosives destroying the tumblers, permanently locking the safe. Also, I need to make a clean bore so that the bit doesn't mistakenly hit anything that may cause the lock to get jammed. My other concern is that if my hole is too wide, anything flammable inside could be set afire by the detonation. I plug the drill into a nearby electrical outlet and position myself so that the bit will go straight in.

Before squeezing the trigger, I push earplugs in my ears and place clear, protective woodworking goggles over my eyes. The drill makes a frighteningly loud whine as it tears into the door to the safe. Thin, metal, curlicue ribbons spiral out and fall on the carpet. As I bear down, smoke comes from between the drill bit and the door. I stop what I'm doing and pull my earplugs out.

"Frank!" I yell.

"What's going on, kid?" comes the response from another part of the office.

"I'm concerned about the smoke!"

Frank walks into the office. "I see what you mean. Walt!" he calls. Using his flashlight, Frank locates the lone smoke detector.

"What's up, boss?" Walt says as he walks into the room

"Get up there and take care of that detector," Frank commands, pointing his flashlight up at the round, white, plastic object with the tiny, red, blinking, electric eye.

Walt grabs a chair from behind one of the desks and wheels it over so that it's directly underneath the device. He puts the end of his small flashlight between his teeth and attempts to stand on the chair, but jumps off as soon it begins to roll out from beneath him. He takes the flashlight out from between his teeth. "Someone's gonna need to hold this chair for me," he says.

Frank groans and slides his flashlight back onto his belt. He grips the seat of the chair as Walt again attempts to stand on it. Frank and I watch Walt examine the smoke detector and the ceiling around it.

"We ain't got all night," Franks hisses.

Walt jumps off the chair. "It's no good," he says. "It's wired into the electrical. If I take it out or attempt to disconnect its power, it may trigger an alert, notifying the fire department. What do you want me to do?"

Frank thinks for a moment, drumming his fingers on the back of the swivel chair. "I've got another idea," he says. From his belt, he pulls out a miniature, motorized contraption no bigger than a magic marker. From a pouch, he takes out a metal fan blade and attaches it to the top of the mechanism and switches it on. "Hold this up to the detector. Hopefully it'll be enough to keep the smoke away." Frank hands the tiny fan to Walt and looks over at me. "Drill away, kid!" he shouts.

I push the earplugs back into my ears and continue to drill. After finishing the first hole, I look over and see Frank holding the chair Walt's standing on as he points the tiny fan just under the detector. They look ridiculous. I begin to laugh.

"Quit laughin' and keep drillin'!" Frank yells, loud enough for me to hear with the earplugs in.

I turn back to the safe and aim the drill at the next orange X. After I've bored the third hole into the safe, I unplug my equipment. I spit on my gloved hand and rub it around the bit. It sizzles. I unscrew it from the drill, put it back in the box, and remove my earplugs and goggles.

Walt jumps off the chair and begins unpacking explosives from his backpack. "You're gonna have to get up there and hold the fan, Jesse," he says.

"Why?" I ask.

"Because as soon as I blow that safe, there's gonna be even more smoke in this office."

"Oh," I say, having not considered this.

"That means you're gonna have to empty it," Frank says to Walt. "I'm gonna have to hold the chair for the kid. Grab the sacks off my belt."

Walt pulls the two long burlap sacks from Frank's belt and throws them around the back of his neck. With the flashlight between his teeth, he begins to ready the detonator and dynamite. "You think these sacks will be big enough to hold everything?" Walt asks Frank while still gripping the flashlight between his teeth.

"I'm betting there's not gonna be enough to fill 'em both," Frank says.

"I sure hope you're wrong," Walt says.

I stand on the chair and hold the small fan next to the smoke detector. I watch as Walt inserts explosives into the holes I've made and clips the detonator to the wicks. He pulls the wire out from its spindle, draping it across the floor and over a desk.

"As soon as that thing blows, unload everything into those sacks. We'll wait until you give us the word, then we'll all shag-ass out the back door. I'm guessing it'll be a matter of seconds before the fire alarm goes off once Jesse isn't holding the fan up to the detector," Frank says.

Walt squats behind a desk and hits the detonator switch. The explosives spark and sizzle nanoseconds before there's a flash and a loud pop. The room is filled with smoke caused by the explosives. Walt runs around the desk. I watch as he quickly becomes surrounded by a thick, white cloud. All I'm able to see is the flashlight between his teeth peering up into the safe and then down into the sack as he unloads everything into the bags. The three of us begin coughing from all the smoke. My eyes water.

After about a half minute, between coughs, Walt shouts, "Okay, she's empty!"

"Grab your shit and let's get outta here!" Frank barks.

I jump off the chair and find my bag on the floor where I'd left it. I pick it up and attempt to get out of the office in the dark. The smoke stings my eyes, and I find that I have to duck down increasingly lower to see the carpeted floor.

The smoke detector goes off, followed by every sprinkler in the building. Walt yells, "Come on!" and from the light in the parking lot, I can see him coughing and holding the backdoor open as smoke pours out. Frank exits first, and I run out just after him.

Walt is holding the two sacks of cash. One appears to be more full than the other. As soon as I'm clear of the backdoor and in the parking lot, he lets the door go and runs to the van. I slide the van's side door open, climbing in with my bag. Walt and Frank get in, and I shut the door. Walt tosses the sacks of cash on the floor in front of Frank, and a second later we're off.

Frank opens the bags and begins counting the money. Walt lights up a cigarette as we drive down the long road out of town.

"Go easy on the gas," Frank says. "I don't want us getting pulled over."

"How much did we get?" I ask.

Frank holds up a fistful of cash. "It's all green, baby!" he says, laughing.

"Woohoo!" Walt yells. He turns on the radio. The Creedence Clearwater Revival song Lookin' Out My Back Door is playing. He turns it up loud and sings along, banging on the steering wheel.

"Don't stop until we're in the parking lot where I picked you guys up," Frank shouts over the music.

I'm tired, but between the cold air coming in from the open passenger window and the loud music, I'm unable to sleep. I lie back on my duffel bag and think about my dad.

I remember his last days with us. Bill said our father was too sensitive for the world. I never understood what that meant. I thought all dads were like ours, quiet and sad. You don't realize until you get older and start working around adults your parent's age that not everybody's the same as the people who raised you. In a way, it was a strange coincidence the way my brother Bill died. Our father also died in a car-related incident.

My mother told us it was an accident. It wasn't until years after the wake and funeral that Bill told me the truth. He'd said dad had lost his job two months before, and he'd driven himself into the side of a concrete highway overpass on purpose. He'd just been notified that he was being investigated for the embezzlement of ten thousand dollars from the company he worked for.

We're on the highway for twenty minutes before Frank orders Walt to pull off at the next rest stop. I get nervous for a reason I can't explain. Walt doesn't say anything, but I can tell from his glances, first at Frank and then at me, in the van's rearview mirror that he wasn't expecting this stop either. Would Frank ditch us and drive away with the loot? Does he have someone waiting at the rest stop to shoot us? Would he hand us over to the police? Walt does as Frank orders and gets off at the next exit. Frank turns the radio off. "Park so you're facing out," he says. Walt turns the van around in the parking lot and backs it into a space. He kills the engine and the lights.

"What are we doing here, Frank?" Walt whispers.

"Waiting," Frank says.

After about ten minutes, a white Cadillac pulls off the highway and into the rest area. The car parks fifteen feet away, facing the van. The Cadillac's lights are on, and the engine is still running. The lights on the car blink twice.

Frank sighs and reaches into one of the burlap sacks. Walt looks nervously from Frank to me and back to Frank. Frank pulls out stacks of bills and then opens the van's glove compartment. He slides out a tan envelope from under the owner's manual, puts the bills inside, and secures it with a metal clip.

"Blink the headlights twice," Frank says.

Walt cautiously reaches up to the panel next to the van's steering wheel and turns the lights on and off twice. Frank opens the passenger door and steps out, shutting it behind him.

The driver side door of the Cadillac opens, and a thin, nervous-looking, middle-aged man with badly receding hair steps out. The man is wearing a plaid shirt and khaki pants with sneakers and a brown leather jacket. A tiny dog wearing a collar and a leash jumps out of the car, barking like crazy. It runs toward Frank and stops halfway between the two men.

"Ferdinand!" the man calls. "Get back here!"

Outside of the van, I see Frank laughing. He walks up to the tiny dog and pets it. He scoops it up in his arms and walks it over to the man. The man shakes his head, looking embarrassed. He opens the rear door of the Cadillac, places the dog on the backseat, and shuts the door.

"What's going on?" I whisper, leaning between the two front seats.

"This must be the guy who gave Frank the tip," Walt says.

Suddenly it all makes sense. The guy probably told his wife he was taking the dog for a walk and drove to a spot Frank and he had agreed to meet after the job was done.

We watch as Frank reaches into his pocket, pulls out the envelope, and hands it to the man. The man doesn't open the envelope. He takes it from Frank, smiles, gets in his car, then drives away.

"He didn't even bother to open it," Walt says.

"For all he knows, there's two books of Pizza Hut coupons in there," I say.

Walt shakes his head. "What a pussy piece of shit".

Frank gets back in the van and shuts the door. "He didn't even bother looking in the envelope before he drove off," he says.

"I was just saying that," Walt says.

"For all he knows, that envelope could be filled with old laundry tickets," Frank says, sighing and shaking his head. "All right, let's get out of here. We'll settle up when we get back to the parking lot."

Back in the parking lot, Frank counts the stacks of cash and slips them into brown envelopes while I use his phone to call a cab. When he's done counting out and divvying up our share of the take, Frank hands the envelopes to Walt and me.
"Count it, boys," he says.

I count out twenty thousand dollars. "Twenty," I say.

"Same," Walt says.

"Is this ten percent of the total take or ten percent of the total after the guy who gave the tip got his cut?" I ask.

"The deal was for ten percent apiece of the total take," Frank says as he collects the remaining cash and loads it into a black leather briefcase.

I look over at Walt and see him trying to do the math.

"Two hundred grand," I say, looking at Walt.

"Huh?" Walt says, looking up from his fingers at me.

"The total take was two hundred thousand," I say.

"I know," Walt says as he shrugs and lights a cigarette.

"A pleasure doing business with you, boys," Frank says. He shuts and locks the briefcase, then shakes our hands.

Walt and I walk out into the parking lot. "What's next for you?" I ask, lighting a cigarette.

"I've got a couple irons in the fire," Walt says coolly as he throws his backpack over his shoulders. "What about you?"

"I'm going to head back home and wait for the phone to ring," I say.

Walt and I watch as the white van pulls out of the parking lot, disappearing down the street.

"I'll ask around," Walt says. "If I find out somebody needs a drill-man, I'll hit you up."

"I appreciate it," I say.

Walt gets on his motorcycle and puts his helmet on. "So, if you and I got twenty grand apiece of the total take that was two hundred thousand, then that means the guy who tipped Frank off got…?"

"Fifty thousand," I say.

"So, then, Frank got…?"

"One hundred and ten thousand," I say.

"Ho-ly shit!"

"It pays to be the boss," I say, shrugging.

"I guess so. We ought to ask for a raise," Walt says. "Vaya con dios!" he shouts as he starts the motorcycle and drives out of the parking lot.

While waiting for my cab, I look at the business card Dawn gave me with her number on it.

BEN

It's late by the time the taxi drops me off at home. I take my bags out of the trunk, pay the driver with cash from the tan envelope, then walk up the front steps of the rented duplex I share with a roommate.

"Yo!" I hear as I'm walking up the steps with my bags.

I look up to see Ben hanging out of our living room window. "Hey!" I yell up. "What are you doing?"

"I just got back from a gig," he says. Ben plays keyboard with a jazz trio at various bars around town. He's smoking a cigarette. "You need a hand?"

"I got it," I say.

He nods and shuts the window, disappearing inside. I drop my duffel bag and suitcase on the porch and unlock the door. With my keys between my teeth, I pick up my bags and walk upstairs. Ben's left the door open. I walk into the living room area, drop my stuff, and sit on the couch.

Ben's sitting in the single chair that came with the couch, watching TV. He's wearing a white tank-top, blue boxer shorts, and black dress socks.

"What is this?" I ask, referring to the TV.

"The Baby. It's fucked up," he says.

On the television is a movie that looks like it was made in the seventies or early eighties. In the scene, there's a party with adults and a full-grown man dressed as an infant.

"You can change it, man," Ben says. "I'm going to bed."

"Goodnight," I say.

"Talk to you tomorrow," he says as he takes his phone off the coffee table and walks out of the living room. As soon as I hear the door to his bedroom close, I take the brown envelope out from my pocket and count my share of the take for a second time.

Ben's never asked too many questions about what I do. Like my mom, he's always assumed I was a traveling locksmith. He was looking for a roommate. The lease and all the utilities are in his name. I'm never late with my share of the rent and bills.

I shut the TV off and carry the duffel bag and suitcase into my bedroom. I drop everything at the foot of my single bed and switch on the lamp on the end table. On my bedroom wall hangs a framed poster from the movie Goodfellas that used to belong to my brother. Next to the movie poster is a framed concert flyer for the band Pavement that features a painting of a naked, curvy black woman with a giant afro. She's laying on her side on an American flag, wearing nothing but a pair of pink boots. She's looking over her shoulder and smiling. This also belonged to my brother. I don't own too much else, just the clothes hanging in my closet, a couple pairs of sneakers, my boots, a few jackets, a couple baseball hats, winter gloves, a stereo, and a guitar.

I turn on the old receiver I have set up on a small cabinet between two modestly-sized speakers. I've Scotch-taped the stereo's antenna, a single wire, to the wall so that I can listen to the local college radio station. I lie down and listen to a man singing a song about it being 1987 all the time.

As I drift off, I imagine buckets of different colored paint being spilled into the ocean off the edge of a boat. The paint creates a cloudy rainbow that sinks and obscures as the boat moves through the water. The nautical imagery fades, and I dream I'm at an airport with Dawn. We're standing on a people mover, side by side. We're both pulling small carry-ons behind us. She's wearing the blue and white bathing suit she was wearing in the hot tub. I look her up and down.

"What?" she asks.

"Will they let you on the plane like that?"

"Why wouldn't they let me on the plane like this?" she asks confusedly. I turn away from her, not wanting to start an argument. We get to the end of the people mover and step off. "I'll just go," she says.

"No...," I start. But it's too late, she's gotten on another people mover, heading in the opposite direction.

I hear barking from inside my carry-on. I open it. Inside, amidst seemingly hundreds of identical blue and white women's bathing suits is Ferdinand, the tiny dog that belonged to the guy who tipped Frank off about the safe in the dealership. I reach down to pick the dog up out of the bag, and he bites the soft webbing between my thumb and pointer finger.

I wake with a start and touch my hand. I immediately feel foolish and throw my legs off the edge of the bed. The stereo is still on. A woman is reading a seemingly endless list of bands, dates, and venues.

I'm hungry. I walk into the kitchen and open the freezer. I take out a frozen pizza and start the oven. I carefully pull the plastic off and set the pie directly on the oven's rack. I don't bother setting a timer. I've made these pizzas so often that I've acquired a sixth sense that tells me when it's done. I think it's a combination of the smell of the dough and the heat of the oven.

I light a cigarette and go through the cabinet beneath the counter where we keep the liquor. I pull out every bottle. I look at all the labels and wonder which liquors I can mix together to make something simple and delicious. In the very back of the cabinet, I find a tiny, red, leather bound bartender's guide. As the pizza heats up, I flip through the book, alternately looking at the labels on the bottles and the guide, but it seems I'm always missing at least one key ingredient of every drink that looks interesting in the book. After a while, I give up and mix a simple gin and tonic in a tall glass with ice. I put all the bottles and the book back into the cabinet.

I sit at our small kitchen table and smoke a cigarette. I take the business card with Dawn's name and number out of my back pocket and stare at it again. I sip the gin and tonic slowly and drum lightly on the table on either side of the business card, staring at it.

I get up from the table and take the pizza out of the oven with the only mitt we have. It's green with a yellow star pattern printed all over it. The thumb of the mitt is torn. If you don't hold a hot pan carefully while wearing it, you'll get burned.

I decide to call Dawn while I let the pizza cool. I take the white cordless phone off the wall and dial the number she gave me. The phone begins to ring on the other end. Her voice mail picks up after five rings, and it's at that moment I realize it's too late at night to be making this call.

"Hi, Dawn, this is Jesse. The, uh, locksmith? I was just calling to let you know I made it back home okay." I cringe at my words. "Um, if you want to call me back, my number is...," I realize I don't have the apartment's phone number memorized. I turn the phone toward me, and fortunately the phone number is written on a tiny strip of white paper that's been slid under the plastic window above the buttons. "...my number *is*, seven, seven, four, six? Yeah, six, um, three, two, two. Anyway," I say, sighing. "Oh! And it's in area code six...," but before I can get the rest of the zip code out, Dawn's voice mail beeps, signaling the end of the time allotted to leave a message. I sigh, hit the power button on the phone, and toss it onto the table. The phone rolls into the middle of the table before stopping, button side up, rocking, like a beetle on its back. I pick up the gin and tonic and drink the rest of it down.

I slide the entire pizza onto a plate, cut it in half twice, and carry it into the living room. I sit on the couch and turn on the TV. I flip through channels, stopping when I recognize the movie Swingers. I've seen it before. It was my brother's favorite. I watch the scene where the Jon Favreau character is trying to leave a voice mail for the girl he met at the party, and he keeps screwing it up and calling her back, making himself sound more and more foolish. Embarrassed for the character and myself, I shut the TV off, eat the entire pizza, and fall asleep in bed with all my clothes on.

The next morning, I'm woken by the sound of male voices and furniture being moved. I roll out of bed and open my door. In the living room, Ben and his drummer, Greg, are moving the couch. Ben's bassist, Jason, is setting up his amp. I wave hello to the guys and light a cigarette.

I walk down the hall and into the kitchen. I dump the cold coffee from the glass carafe into the sink and refill it with fresh water from the faucet. I pour the water into the back of the machine and fill a new paper cone with fresh grounds.

I walk back into the living room and look around. Ben and Greg have moved the couch over by the window and walked downstairs to get the rest of the gear. I sit down on the couch and watch Jason tune his bass.

"How's it goin', man?" he asks.

"Been worse," I say, shrugging. I get up to walk back into the kitchen. "You want some coffee?" I ask Jason.

"Nah, man, I'm good, thanks," he says as he runs his nimble fingers up and down the frets.

I take a mug out of the cabinet and pour myself a cup. On the table, I find a glass sugar dispenser that looks like it came from a diner and pour just enough into my coffee to make it sweet. I take a small container of half and half out of the fridge, smell it to make sure it hasn't spoiled, and add enough so that there's about two centimeters of space between the coffee and the lip of the mug. I hear Ben and Greg coming up the stairs. I open the door. They walk in, carrying Greg's drum kit.

I sit down at the table and drink the coffee. All three guys walk through the kitchen, heading downstairs to collect the rest of the drums. After I've finished my coffee and cigarette, Ben and his band have got almost everything set up.

As I shower, I first hear Ben's keyboard before the other two musicians join in. The muffled sound of gentle jazz through the door is invigorating. I wash my hair and rinse out the suds. I open the door to get the full effect of my roommate's trio's music as I dry myself. I wrap a towel around my waist and walk back into my bedroom. I leave the door open as I pull on clean boxers, cargo shorts, and an old Iron Maiden tour t-shirt. It was from the first concert my brother Bill ever took me to and remarkably it still fits. My ears rang for at least three days after that show.

I take a triangle-shaped, green, glass ashtray off my nightstand and walk into the living room. I sit on the couch and light another cigarette. The guys sound good. Ben smiles as each guy takes a turn soloing. After I finish my second cigarette of the day, I go back into my bedroom and take a pair of old, white, shell-toed sneakers out of my closet. I put them on over athletic socks.

I find my keys and wallet and drop them into my pockets. I take my motorcycle helmet off the top of the refrigerator and head downstairs. It's about a twenty-minute ride to my mom's house from our apartment. I take the highway and then back roads.

After dad died, mom continued to park her car on the same side she'd always had. I pull into the space my father's car used to occupy. The front door to the house is unlocked. Mom is at the kitchen table, reading a People magazine.

"Hey," I say.

She takes off her glasses and smiles. I walk over and give her a hug. She gives me a kiss on the cheek. "Do you want anything before you start?" she asks.

"You got any bagels?"

"There should be some in the basket next to the microwave." I take an egg bagel out of a plastic bag filled with bagels from the supermarket bakery and begin eating it like a donut. "Don't you want it toasted?" my mother asks.

I shake my head and look at the bagel. "This is fine," I say. "Does the mower need gas?"

"You were the last one to use it."

"I can't remember," I say.

"How was your trip?"

"It was fine."

"Did you get any time to yourself, or were you working the whole time?"

"I got a little bit of time to myself. The motel they put us up at had a pool. I went for a swim. Met a girl."

"A girl?" my mother says, sitting back.

"Yeah, I helped her with her car door and she bought me a coffee," I say, shrugging and smiling.

"Oh, well, do you think you'll see her again?"

"I wouldn't mind," I say, taking a bite of the bagel.

"What does she do?"

"Um, she's a manager at a clothing store."

"Oh?"

I nod and take another bite of the bagel, looking anywhere but at my mother.

"Any store I'd know?" my mother asks.

"It's called…Maxine's? Does that sound right?"

My mother looks puzzled and shakes her head.

"Maybe that's not what it's called. I can't remember," I say.

I roll my mother's push mower out of the shed. I get about half the lawn done before it runs out of gas. I push it back to the shed to fill it up from the can my dad always kept in there, emptying it.

"Jesse!" my mom calls from the deck. I walk closer so she doesn't have to yell. She holds up a glass. "You want some lemonade?"

"Yeah, okay," I say.

I sit on the steps and drink the lemonade. My mom sits down next to me.

"So, what was this girl's name?"

"Dawn," I say.

"Does she live nearby?"

"The number she gave me had an area code I didn't recognize."

"Have you called her?"

"Yeah, but I just left a message on her voice mail."

My mother's quiet for a moment as she watches me drink the last of the lemonade from the glass.

"Well, you know, if you want to, you can always invite her over here for dinner. I love to cook, and I wouldn't do anything to embarrass you…too much."

I laugh. "I'll let you know, mom," I say, standing up and handing her the glass.

After I finish mowing my mother's lawn, I find myself thinking about Dawn. I'm wondering if she heard my message and if she'll call me back.

"I'm gonna take off, mom!" I yell through the screen door. "Everything's back in the shed," I say as she comes out onto the deck. I give her a hug and she holds me longer than usual. "You alright?" I ask.

"Please take care of yourself, okay?"

"I will," I say.

My mom lets me go. I pick up my helmet from the seat of the motorcycle and put it on. "I hate that bike," she whispers. I don't say anything. "Be safe," she says. I wave goodbye as I start the bike and pull out of the driveway and onto the street.

When I get back to my place, I park my motorcycle next to Jason's SUV. The drums are all locked safely inside, signifying the end of another rehearsal. I walk upstairs, my helmet in hand, and open the door. The three guys are standing in the kitchen. Jason's got his bass in a bag over his shoulder and his amplifier at his feet.

"Hey, man," Ben says as I enter.

"Hey," I say as I put my helmet on top of the refrigerator and open the door, taking out a bottle of water.

"We'll see you later, Ben. Take care, Jesse," Greg says as he and Jason walk downstairs.

I wave at the two guys as I take a sip from the water bottle.

"You got a call," Ben says as he hands me a notepad from off the table.

I look at the name and number. Walt. I can't help but feel slightly disappointed.

"Thanks," I say, pulling off the top sheet of the notepad with Walt's name and number on it. I push the paper into my pocket and toss the pad back on the table. I put the water back in the fridge before I take the phone off the wall and walk into my room with it, shutting the door behind me. I dial Walt's number and wait for him to pick up.

"Yo!" he says upon answering.

"Hey, Walt, it's Jesse," I say.

"Jesse!" he says. I can tell he's smiling.

"Where are you?" I ask.

"Home. Got in pretty late last night, but it's not like I've got anybody waiting up for me or anything. Hey, listen, the reason I called was because I've got a job opportunity I think you might be interested in."

"You need a...?" I begin to ask.

"I'd rather not talk about it over the phone," Walt says, cutting me off mid-sentence. "Do you know where the House of Stacks is?"

"The pancake place? Yeah, I know where it is."

"Meet me there tomorrow morning at nine."

"I'll be there," I say.

THE HOUSE OF STACKS

I pull into the House of Stacks just after nine. I recognize Walt's motorcycle and park mine next to it. It's a sunny morning without too much wind. It's supposed to rain later, but right now it's perfect motorcycle-riding weather.

Walt's outside the restaurant, sitting on a bench next to a newspaper dispenser. He's wearing sunglasses, a leather jacket, black jeans, boots, and a white t-shirt with a Bud Light logo on it. His helmet is next to him on the bench like a disembodied head. He doesn't bother to stand as I approach. I'm wearing blue jeans and a black Slipknot t-shirt.

Walt nods at me and lights a cigarette. From the way he's positioned on the bench, and the placement of his helmet, there's no room for me to sit. I hold my helmet by the mouth guard at my side.

"What's up?" he says.

"Hey," I say.

"You live nearby?"

"Not too far."

There's no way I'm going to tell Walt where I live. If there's one thing my brother Bill taught me when he was getting involved in the whole safe-drilling gig, it's that you want to keep any of the guys you might work with at arm's length. Bill had heard stories from Frank about fellas showing up, looking for places to "lay low" for a while, and the next thing the accommodating party knew, they were hauled in for questioning for harboring a criminal. Those lucky enough to avoid that hassle still got an uninvited roommate for weeks, if not months.

"You spend your cut?" Walt asks, referring to the money we'd made on the job.

"Nah," I say. "You?"

"I got rid of some debt," he says, looking away.

"Yeah?"

Walt clears his throat. "Yeah, I owed a couple guys upstate. They got their dough, but they also let me know they don't like late payments." Walt lifts his sunglasses. The skin under his left eye is dark purple.

"Ouch!"

"I've had worse," he says, taking a drag off his cigarette and wincing slightly. From the way Walt says it, I know he's not kidding.

I get tired of standing and put my helmet on the ground, sitting on it. I can't decide if Walt's bench-hogging is due to ignorance or if it's some kind of power trip. The smell of pancakes wafting by every time the restaurant door opens is making me too hungry to care either way.

"That your bike?" he asks.

I turn around to look at it. "Yup."

Walt nods. "You can afford something nicer than that, can't ya?" he asks with a smile. "Why don't you get yourself a Katana or a Harley?"

"I've had that one for a couple years now," I say. "Kinda got attached to it. You know what I mean?"

Walt stares at me and slowly shakes his head. "No, I don't know what you mean," he says. "I never get attached to anything."

"Nothing?"

Walt drops his cigarette, stomping it out with his boot, even though there's a trashcan with an ash tray built into the lid just a couple feet away. "I never get attached to bikes, cars, women, jobs…bosses."

"What about friends?" I ask.

"Friends? Well that depends on what you mean by friends. See, some folks will say they're your friend and they're really just acquaintances. You know what the difference between a friend and an acquaintance is, Jesse?" I don't say anything. "A friend is someone you can tell anything to. And when I say anything, I mean you can tell that person *anything*. Even your darkest fantasies. Maybe you like to jack off your dog." I start laughing. Walt smiles a tiny bit. When he doesn't laugh, I start to feel uncomfortable and clear my throat. "I'm serious," Walt says. "Maybe you like to stick your pinky finger in your cat's asshole." Again, I start laughing uncomfortably. "I ain't saying cats like it, and I ain't saying they don't. You see, Jesse, we're not friends, so I wouldn't tell you whether I know if cats like a pinky in their stinky or not." I stop laughing. Walt's no longer smiling. I can't see his eyes through his aviators, but I know he's staring at me. "Friend's a person you can

46

tell anything, that's my point," Walt licks his lips and turns toward two teen girls walking between us. I look down. Walt rubs his lips with his thumb. He stares until the two girls are inside the restaurant and the door closes behind them, then he turns back toward me. "I'm sorry, Jesse," Walt says, picking up his helmet and putting it on his lap. "You want to sit on the bench?" At this point, I don't want to be any closer to Walt than I am now.

"I'm cool," I say.

"You're cool," Walt says, smiling and nodding. "Where was I?"

"Friends and acquaintances," I say.

"Oh, yeah, right. So, like I said, friends are folks you can tell anything to and not worry about being judged, or them running and telling everyone on God's green earth what you been up to behind closed doors. Acquaintances, on the other hand…acquaintances you can joke around with and maybe you ask for advice now and again, or maybe you give advice when they ask for it, but you keep them at a distance. That's you and me, Jesse. Acquaintances. Would you agree?"

"Sure," I shrug. At this point, I swear I can hear my stomach growl, and I'm beginning to believe Walt and I will be sitting outside of this restaurant for the rest of our lives.

"Now, I would love for us to be friends, Jesse. Being friends would mean I could tell you anything without having to worry about you judging me or you running to tell your mother or your cousins or someone we both know…like Frank."

I move around uncomfortably on the motorcycle helmet. I'm starting to get the feeling Walt's palms are itchy for the kind of money a boss like Frank can take away from a job like the one we just pulled. I don't care for the direction this conversation is headed, and I don't want Walt to feel like he can trust me with information that might put my criminal career in jeopardy. I'm suddenly wishing Walt would go back to the less uncomfortable topic of creepy personal information that you can trust a friend with.

An elderly couple slowly pushes the restaurant's door open from the inside as they exit. I see an opportunity and immediately stand and pick my helmet up. I open the door wide for the old folks.

The man nods a thank you as he and his wife slowly walk out into the morning light.

"Gentleman Jesse!" Walt says, standing and laughing.

"That's me, I guess," I say.

I walk into the restaurant after the couple is clear of the doorway, Walt follows. A guy wearing a filthy apron, who doesn't look like he's out of high school, sits us in an empty booth in the back and promptly pours us coffees without asking whether we want them or not. He drops a handful of creamers from inside his apron's front pocket in the center of the table. I open the menu and immediately begin speaking my thought process as I'm looking at the food. My hope is Walt won't start up his conversation about who he trusts to share information with regarding his monetary aspirations.

"I was thinking I'd get an omelet, but after smelling those pancakes, I'm thinking maybe I'll go that route. Or, maybe I'll try the French toast. Haven't had French toast in a while…"

"Jesse," Walt says.

"Hmmm?" I say without looking up from my menu.

"Pass me the sugar, would you?"

"Sure," I say. I put down my menu and slide the small, white, ceramic boat of sugar packets across the table.

"I'm setting up a job," Walt says flatly. "I need a drill-man."

I clear my throat. I pull back the thin peel-away tops on two of the mini creamers left by the guy with the filthy apron and pour them into my mug.

"You mind passing me that sugar, Walt?" He sighs and slowly slides the sugar toward my side of the table. I reach out to take the sugar and Walt holds it firmly, not letting me have it. I look up. He takes off his sunglasses and looks me dead in the eyes. "You ever coordinate and pull a job on your own before, Walt?" I ask.

"First person to jump out of an airplane never did it before," Walt says.

"What the hell does that mean?" I whisper.

Walt lets the sugar go, and I slide it over to my side of the table. I take out two packets and shake them a few times before ripping them open.

"This job's going to happen whether you're in or not," he says. "I just figured I'd give you first dibs, because you're reliable and we get along okay."

A waitress comes to our table, and Walt leans back and sighs.

"Welcome to the House of Stacks. My name's Mindy, and I'll be your server today," the perky blonde says as she pulls a notepad out of her apron pocket. "What can I get you this morning?"

Walt grunts and mutters, "I'm still deciding."

"Do you need more time? I can come back," Mindy says.

"No," Walt says sharply. "Take his order. I'll know what I want in a second."

"I'll have the Half Stack," I say. "With a bagel and cream cheese on the side, please."

"Bring me the same thing, except with a side of bacon," Walt says as he closes his menu and hands it to the girl without looking at her.

I can tell my hesitation to say yes to Walt's offer isn't sitting well. He doesn't even bother ogling our waitress as she walks away.

"Listen, Walt, I'm sure whatever you've got planned is going to go great, and I'm sure I'll regret not saying yes…"

"You know what?" Walt interrupts. "It's not a big deal. I've got another drill-man in mind anyway."

"Oh…," I start.

"Yeah, I mean, I just figured that since I was in town I'd offer it to you first. I mean, because that's the kind of guy I am."

"Right, I appreciate it," I say, lying.

Walt clears his throat. There's an awkward silence between us. I drum nervously on the table and try not to make eye contact.

"I think I'm going to use the rest of my share of the money from the last job and take a vacation this summer," Walt says before taking a sip of coffee.

"Nice. Where are you thinking of going?" I ask, even though I really don't care but want desperately to break the tension between us.

"I've never been to Jamaica," he says.

"I've heard it's beautiful there," I say.

"Hey, since you're not interested in being in the crew I'm putting together, how would you feel about loaning me your equipment? I mean, I'll pay you for the rental…"

"Uh," I start. "Listen." I clear my throat and move around uncomfortably in the booth. I pause, drumming my fingers on my motorcycle helmet next to me. "The equipment I use belonged to my brother, and I really don't feel comfortable letting anyone else use it, you know what I mean?"

Walt nods and sighs. "Sure, I get that," he says. "You know, Jesse, I knew your brother."

"Yeah?"

"Yeah, I was on that last job with him before he had the accident," Walt says, shaking his head. "Damn shame what happened to Billy. He ever mention me?"

"No," I say flatly.

"Your brother was a good drill-man. He trusted me."

"Oh yeah?" I say.

"Mmm hmm," Walt nods. "Billy would've trusted me with his equipment."

I sigh. If there's anything I knew about my brother, it's that he hated anyone calling him "Billy" and Walt is exactly the kind of sleezeball Bill would have been wary of. I know without a doubt my brother wouldn't have loaned his equipment to anyone, least of all someone like Walt.

Our waitress comes to the table, carrying two plates.

"Half Stack with a bagel," she says.

"That's me," I say.

"And the Half Stack with bacon," she says, putting the plate down in front of Walt.

"Uh, what's this?" Walt asks, pointing at his plate and looking disgustedly at our waitress.

"Oh, is that not what you ordered?" she asks.

Walt guffaws. "I asked for the Half Stack with a side of sausage," he says sternly.

"Oh, okay, no problem," our waitress says as she begins to lift Walt's plate away.

"You heard me order the sausage, right?" Walt says to me.

"Uh, I thought you said bacon, but maybe I'm just picturing bacon because it's all I can smell," I say, even though I'm positive Walt ordered bacon.

"It's no problem," the waitress says. "I'll get this fixed for you right away."

As she turns to head back into the kitchen, Walt says, "You know what? Don't fix it. I'll just eat the bacon."

"Are you sure?" Mindy asks.

"Yeah, it's fine. But you know what really bugs me? What really bugs me is you didn't even say sorry for messing up my order," Walt says as he takes the plate from the waitress and begins pouring syrup over his pancakes.

"Oh, I'm so sorry, sir," the waitress says.

"Well, now you're just being sarcastic," Walt says, slamming down the syrup.

"No, I...," the waitress stammers as she begins to defend herself.

"You know what? Get me your manager," Walt says, shaking his head.

The waitress turns without another word and disappears into the kitchen.

"You believe that shit?" he asks, shaking his head.

I shake my head and take a bite of my bagel.

The manager, a bald man who looks to be in his forties, comes to our table.

"I understand you weren't happy with the service, sir," the man says to Walt.

"Uh, yeah," Walt says. "Firstly, our waitress brings me the wrong breakfast, and then she doesn't apologize."

"Let me try to make this right. Your breakfast is on us today," the manager says.

"What about his?" Walt asks, pointing to my plate.

"Uh...," the manager starts.

"Mine's fine," I say.

"Is there anything else I can help you with today, sir?" the manager asks Walt.

Walt pauses for an uncomfortably long moment, sighs, and says, "No." The manager turns and walks away. Walt shakes his head. "You know, you could've had a free breakfast if you'd have just kept your mouth shut," Walt says. I shrug and continue eating.

I pay for breakfast. Walt tells me not to leave a tip, but I do anyway when he's not looking.

We get on our motorcycles in the parking lot. I put my helmet on and start my bike.

"Hey!" I hear him shout over the roar of the engines. I look over, and Walt's holding his fist out. "Don't leave me hangin', bro'!"

I reluctantly give Walt a fist bump without looking at him, and we pull out of the parking lot. Walt turns, heading in the opposite direction of myself. I think about whether I'd ever drill for anyone other than Frank. The thought of making a ton of dough on a bigger job is somewhat enticing, but I can't ever imagine working for Walt.

When I get home, I fold laundry while listening to the radio. I think about what Walt said about friends and acquaintances. I realize it's been a while since I hung out with anyone I graduated high school with. I don't know if this means that we've went from being friends to acquaintances or if they were acquaintances all along. I don't know if I'd trust any one of them with a secret. I can't imagine them understanding what I've been doing to make money since my brother died.

After I finish putting away my laundry, I pull my acoustic guitar out from under the bed, another hand-me-down from my big brother, another part of my inheritance. I only know a few chords, but I strum away and sing the Beach Boys' song Sloop John B from the songbook Bill left in the case. After strumming a bit too aggressively, a string breaks, and I decide it's a sign I should quit for the day. I put the guitar back in the case with the broken string still attached and slide it under the bed.

I find bacon in the refrigerator's crisper drawer and begin to make myself a BLT for lunch. As the bacon heats up in the pan, I wash and slice a tomato and a head of lettuce. The bacon is just starting to sizzle, and I'm patting the lettuce dry with a paper towel, when the phone rings. I pick it up, cradling it between my shoulder and chin as I gently lift the bacon strips with a pair of metal tongs and flip them over.

"Hello?"

"Hi, is Jesse there?" a female voice says.

"This is Jesse."

"Hey, it's Dawn."

"Oh! Hey!" I say, excited that she's called.

"I got your message, but you didn't leave me the area code," she says.

"Oh yeah, I realized I'd forgot to include it just before your voice mail cut me off. How did you figure it out?"

"Well, you did get in the number six before my phone stopped recording. It didn't take too much detective work to figure out where you were. I actually got it on the first try."

"Thanks for calling me back," I say.

"So," she says.

"So," I say.

"How have you been?"

"I've been okay. Just doing some laundry, playing a little guitar. I'm cooking right now."

"Really?"

"Yeah," I say.

"What are you making?"

"Bacon."

"Oh! Anybody can do that!" she says, laughing.

"Okay, well, that's what I'm making. It still counts as cooking, doesn't it?"

"Yeah, I guess. Kind of a late breakfast, isn't it?"

"Lunch, actually," I say.

"Bacon for lunch?"

"I'm making a BLT."

"Ooh, I haven't had a BLT in a long time. You put mayo on yours?"

"Of course," I say.

"Do you toast the bread?"

"Absolutely. You?"

"I wouldn't have it any other way."

"What'd you do for lunch?" I ask.

"Um, I cooked some very lovely macaroni and cheese," she says, and I can tell she's smiling when she says it.

"Oh, you cooked some *very lovely* macaroni and cheese, did you?" I say, laughing.

"Oh, come on!" She says. "If making bacon counts as cooking, making macaroni and cheese *definitely* counts as cooking," she says.

"Well, I guess that depends on if you *made* it, or if you boiled a pot of water and opened a box."

She sighs. "Anyway," she says, trying to change the topic.

"Well, which is it?" I ask, smiling into the receiver.

"Did you say you were playing guitar?"

"Oh, come on! Don't change the subject. If you can give me a hard time about me calling making bacon *cooking*, then I deserve to know what kind of macaroni and cheese you made.

She sighs again. "Yeah, it was out of the box, but that doesn't mean I can't cook real macaroni and cheese with the breadcrumbs and everything!"

"Aha!" I say, laughing. "Homemade mac and cheese with breadcrumbs sounds really good."

"Well, maybe someday I'll make it for you."

"Yeah?" I ask.

"If you're lucky," she says.

"Oh, if I'm lucky, okay."

We both laugh.

"But back up for real," she says.

"What?"

"You play guitar?"

"It's my brother's old acoustic. I just mess around with it. Do you play any instruments?"

"I used to play flute and then saxophone for a few years. I played up through junior high, and then I stopped in high school."

"What made you stop? Did you get bored with it?" I ask.

"No, I loved playing the saxophone. It just wasn't cool when I got to high school. The band kids were made fun of."

"Isn't that a shame?"

"What, kids making fun of other kids?"

"Well, that you gave something up that you loved because it wasn't considered cool."

"Doesn't mean I can't go back to it."

"True," I say.

"So, when are we going to get together again, Jesse?"

I sigh. "I don't know. Sooner rather than later, I hope."

"I'm supposed to get my work schedule for the next two weeks this Friday. Why don't we talk then and make a plan to meet up?"

"Okay, that sounds good. Should I call you, or do you want to call me?"

"Well, you're the one without a mobile phone, so I'm going to suggest you call me. I mean, I don't go anywhere without my phone, you're the one who has to be at a certain place at a certain time to make or take a call. Why don't you have a phone again?"

"I don't know."

"Bad credit?"

"Come on!" I say. "I really don't have a reason…I'm old fashioned?"

"Okay, grandpa!" she says, laughing. "We'll talk next Friday. Think of something fun for us to do."

"I will," I say. "Have a good night."

"You, too."

I take the bacon out of the pan, lay it on some paper towels, fold the paper over the bacon, and blot at it until the towel is soaked with grease. I build myself a BLT on toasted bread with mayonnaise, and then I take the sandwich downstairs and sit on the front steps, eating it while watching the neighborhood kids. A few little black girls are playing jump rope. Some boys are riding their bikes down the street. The sandwich hits the spot. I try to imagine Dawn as a young girl playing the saxophone.

WALT CALLS

I accompany my roommate and his band at a tiny martini bar downtown called Tini's. I help Ben unload the drums and carry them inside the venue.

As Ben and his band play, I sit at the bar with a martini made with Hendrick's gin and lemon juice. I sip the eight-dollar drink slowly and try to make it last. I applaud after each solo, but I can't say my ear is refined enough to tell if one performer is more technically proficient at his instrument than another.

Behind the bar, I notice a safe, which the bartender unknowingly reveals to me as he opens a lower cabinet to make change. I immediately recognize it as a Mosler, one of America's oldest and most trusted brands.

"I saw what you have there," I say to the bartender when he turns around.

"Pardon?" the man says. He looks to be in his mid-fifties, fat, with receding red hair and a goatee.

"Your little box in the cabinet," I say. I'm not drunk, but I'm feeling confident.

"Oh, the safe?" he asks.

"That's right," I say.

"Yeah, it's old. Boss won't part with it. It's like furniture at this point, the thing's so heavy."

"What does he keep in there?" I ask.

"I don't know," the bartender says.

I nod and drink my martini.

After the gig, I help Ben and his bandmates load up their equipment. I ride home on my motorcycle and meet the trio outside the duplex. I help carry Ben's keyboard and amplifier upstairs. After everything is inside, the phone rings.

"Hello?"

"Jesse?" a man's voice says wearily.

"Yes, this is Jesse."

The man's words come slowly. "Things didn't go as well as expected."

"Who is this?"

There's a long moment before the tired man's voice says, "Walt."

My blood turns to ice in my veins. I turn to see Ben staring at me quizzically. "Oh! Walt, yes, sorry to hear that," I say as I look at Ben, nodding and smiling. Ben shrugs and walks down the hall toward his bedroom.

"Jesse," he says.

"I'm here," I say.

"I got us out with our lives, but just barely."

"How many guys?

"Three including me."

"I'm guessing I shouldn't ask for details," I say.

"I'm not mentioning locations or specifics regarding the job over the phone," he says. Walt swallows, and I hear what sounds like liquid falling into a bottle. There's a pause.

"You gonna make it?" I ask.

"I'll make it, but I'm never doing a job with an unprepared team again. Anyway, I could've used you tonight."

"Was it worth it at all?"

"No, but fortunately I have enough left over from the last job to pay these guys something, because we didn't get anything."

"Nothing?"

"Nada. I can kiss that Jamaican vacation goodbye."

I sigh, as I remember sitting on my helmet outside the pancake restaurant and essentially being held hostage by Walt and his rant on friendship. I suddenly don't want to be on the phone with him any longer. Fortunately, he begins to wrap up our conversation.

"I've got to go change this bandage," he says.

"Right, well, keep your chin up, man," I say. "Let me know if you hear of any other jobs coming down the pipe."

"I will," Walt says. "Peace."

"Peace," I say and hang up. Peace, I think to myself. What the fuck's peaceful about any of this?

I brush my teeth, take off my clothes, and get into bed. I turn on the radio and fall asleep to the sound of two teenagers discussing college sports.

I dream that I'm on an airplane, flying to Las Vegas. My brother is in the seat next to me. He's smiling and looking out the window.

"You gonna gamble when we get there?" I ask.

"I think I'm gonna gamble," Bill replies, nodding and smiling.

I look down. On my lap is the songbook Bill left in the guitar case. I go to put the book into the pocket on the back of the seat in front of me and a photo of Dawn falls out. In the photo, she's sitting on a chaise lounge, wearing the same bathing suit she was wearing when I first met her. She's smiling and looking at the camera through heart-shaped sunglasses. Bill looks over.

"Who's the girl?" he asks.

"Her name's Dawn," I say. I put the photo back inside the book and push it into the pocket of the seat.

"You gonna gamble?"

"Yeah," I say, nodding. "I think I'm gonna gamble."

A WAGON FILLED WITH PROBLEMS

I walk to a supermarket downtown. The store's a good two miles away, but it's a clear day, and I can use the exercise. On the way, I smoke my last two cigarettes. I walk by a park with a small outdoor stage and see a group of twentysomethings loudly rehearsing what sounds like Shakespeare. Some are in shorts, but most are wearing jeans and t-shirts. They're all holding scripts and working out their places on the stage. A few pairs of performers are quietly running lines with one another in the wings.

Just beyond the park, I spy a young man and woman making out behind a tree where they can't be seen by the acting troupe. White sheets of paper blow around on the lawn, but the couple takes no notice as they continue to kiss and hold each other with their eyes closed.

I try to remember the last time I kissed a woman. It must have been over a year ago. I was at a club called Shooter's with Ben and one of his bandmates. I had never been to the club before, and the music they played wasn't the jazz I always associated with my roommate and his trio.

I'd had at least four beers within the span of an hour and a half. I don't normally drink that much that fast, and I was feeling it. I would have never danced to music like the stomping electronic garbage being played by the young DJ behind the riser, but, like I said, I was feeling good, and I was trying to make the best of the situation.

A woman with straight brown hair parted in the middle, wearing a tight, black tank top and dark green shorts with heels danced up to me. We were moving together very closely. She appeared to be Hispanic, but it was too dark in the club to really tell. She had brown eyes and a nice smile.

I asked if I could buy her a drink. I had to practically yell it into her ear since the music was so loud. She couldn't understand what I was asking, so I made a motion with my hand of drinking a beverage. She nodded, and we made our way off the dance floor and to the bar area in the back of the club, further away from the speakers where the music wasn't as loud. I asked if she wanted a beer and she said, "Water." I ordered two.

I asked her some questions about herself, but could only understand about half of her answers. I just kept smiling and nodding. Finally, I asked her if she wanted to make out. She shrugged and said sure. I leaned in to kiss her and she leaned away, laughing. I said, "I'm sorry. I thought you said you wanted to." She said she did, but just not at the bar.

We went outside and kissed for a long time against the brick wall of the club. Although it got to a point where I wanted more, my hands never strayed beyond her back and shoulders. At one point, she pushed me away. I first thought it was because I was being too aggressive, but I realized it was because her phone was vibrating. She pulled it out of her back pocket and looked at it. She was, like, "Oh shit, I gotta go. My friends are ready to leave, and they're wondering where I am." Before I could even say, 'Can I call you?' she was back inside. I lit a cigarette and smoked half of it before Ben and his bandmate walked out of the club and said they were ready to leave.

When we got back, Ben made popcorn on the stove. He said that at one point he saw me dancing with a brunette in a black tank top. I just nodded.

I walk across the parking lot of the supermarket. I see a man walking in the opposite direction, holding a little boy by the arm, pulling him along. The man is shouting angrily into a cell phone. I make out some of the words. Most of them are obscenities. The man's son looks to be no more than three-years-old. Other than curses, the only other words I can make out are, "I shouldn't have to drop him off...," and "This wasn't part of our arrangement...," and "Well I guess I'll be speaking with my attorney then...." I gather the man is arguing with the boy's mother and that he's bringing their son to the mother's house against the plans he'd previously made. I feel bad for the little boy stumbling along, his arm held high as his father yanks at him while yelling into the phone as if the father's pulling a wagon filled with problems. Nobody else in the parking lot seems to notice the father and the little boy.

I walk inside the grocery store and take a small, red basket from a stack near the door. As I walk up and down the aisles, I recognize the Traveling Wilburys' song End of the Line playing over the store's speakers. Tom Petty is singing about not caring about the kind of car he drives. I try to imagine what kind of car Tom Petty drives. I picture something better than what most folks have, but maybe to Tom Petty his car's just okay because he's had money a long time and no longer has a sense of modesty or knowledge of what folks without a lot of money drive. Or maybe Tom Petty didn't write the lyrics. Who the fuck knows?

In the frozen food section, I pick up a couple pizzas and put them in my basket. I notice an old man struggling to open a freezer door on the other side of the aisle. I walk over and pull the door open for him. "Thanks," he says in a weak-sounding voice. I ask him if he needs help with any of the other freezer doors. He slowly walks down the aisle, looking through the glass. I follow alongside. He turns to me and shakes his head.

I walk down the bread aisle and pick up a loaf of wheat. In the produce aisle, I pick up more tomatoes and lettuce for BLTs.

I wait in the checkout line behind a middle-aged woman with a small red basket like the one I'm holding. The woman is wearing a dress with an orange and black flower pattern and white sneakers that appear to only ever be worn after a long day in less comfortable, formal shoes. I assume she's come directly from work. I wonder what she's going home to. I look in her basket to try to get an idea of what her life is like. I see a bottle of white wine, a box of Ritz crackers, a block of cheddar cheese, a few cups of Greek yogurt, a single roll of toilet paper, and a quart of store brand chocolate ice cream.

The young cashier has a badge that says Ashlee. Underneath her name are the words TWO YEARS, signifying how long she's been working at the supermarket. Her dyed black hair is pulled back in a ponytail. She's wearing eye makeup that sits in tiny, black chunks atop fake-looking lashes. The sleeves of her maroon supermarket smock are rolled up to the middle of her forearms, which look unhealthily thin. I watch as her bony fingers with lingering, chipped, light blue nail polish pick up the middle-aged woman's items and run them over a scanner.

The song Lotta Love is playing over the store's speakers. It's the version with the woman singing. For a while I thought this was the only version until I heard Neil Young's original late one night on the local college radio station.

An old, heavyset black woman with a scarf wrapped around her head bags the middle-aged white woman's groceries. The woman in the sneakers takes a wallet from her purse and opens it, sliding a twenty and a ten-dollar bill out. She pays the cashier, takes her change, and places it all in her purse before picking up her bagged items, nodding to the black woman, and leaving the store.

"Hi, how are you today?" Ashlee asks me robotically. She can't be more than eighteen.

"I'm okay, thanks," I say. I consider for a moment asking her how she is, but I honestly don't care, and I just want to get out of the store. "Could I also get a pack of Marlboros?" I ask.

Ashlee turns and takes a pack of cigarettes out of the cabinet behind her and runs them over the scanner.

"Do you want to hold onto these?" she asks.

"Yeah, thank you," I say, taking the cigarettes from her thin digits and putting them in the chest pocket of my shirt.

I watch as the girl scans each one of my items: two frozen pizzas, lettuce, tomatoes, mayonnaise, bacon, wheat bread, eggs, milk, butter, and a bottle of grape soda. I pay for my stuff and walk out of the supermarket. In the parking lot, I stop, put my bags down, and light a cigarette. I hold my groceries in one hand so I can keep the other hand free to hold the butt.

On my walk home, I pass two boys skateboarding on a corner near a stone bench and a flagpole. They each take turns jumping onto the bench, landing the back wheels of their skateboards on the edge of the bench's seat, and then jumping off.

I remember back to the time I begged a friend to let me ride his skateboard down a hill. He told me I should practice on level ground before I try, but I was convinced that I could do it because I'd observed him long enough. He finally relented. I was halfway down the steep incline before the board began to wobble from side to side. I leaned back in an attempt to regain control, and the thing flew out from beneath my feet. I fell, landing on my ass before rolling backward, my head hitting the pavement hard. I didn't get a concussion, but I did get a painful lump. That was the first and last time I tried something like that.

When I pass by the park where the young people were rehearsing, I notice only a few of the original troupe are left onstage. The couple who were making out under the tree are gone. There are a few sheets of paper still in the grass. I walk over and bend down to get a better look at the script. The character's names appear to be Shakespearean, but I can't identify the play.

I unload my groceries and make myself an afternoon coffee. I take a mug outside, sit on the steps, smoke a cigarette, and watch kids play in the street.

The afternoon moves into the evening. I lie in bed, listening to a jazz show on the receiver. From the kitchen, I hear the phone ring. Ben answers it. Moments later, he's knocking on my door. I get up and open it.

"Hey, man, it's for you," he says, handing me the cordless receiver.

"Hello?" I say.

"Jesse," a familiar voice says.

"Frank?"

"I've got another opportunity. Same area as the last job. I'll put you up at the motel, and we can work out all the details in the abandoned office building across the street. Are you in?"

I sit on the edge of my bed and run my hand through my hair. "How many other guys on the job?"

"Same crew," Frank says. "Are you in?" he asks a second time.

I really don't want to work with Walt again. I think back to what he'd insinuated about Frank and the amount of money that Frank walked away with after the last job.

"What's the cut look like?" I ask.

"I can't say for certain, but It'll be at least as much as last time, if not more."

I remember my conversation with Dawn. I'm wondering if she would want to meet up at the motel. After all, it's familiar territory. We could swim and go to the coffee shop across the street again. The thought of getting together with her is more appealing than the job opportunity. I decide to take a chance on Dawn agreeing to meet up with me and tell Frank I'll do the job.

"I'm in. When would you need me?" I ask.

"I'm not going to get into it over the phone. I've put letters in the mail to both yourself and Walt with specifics regarding the dates, times, and locations. I'd appreciate it if you'd give me a call as soon as you've had a chance to look it over. I need to lock things down on my end."

"You got it," I say.

"Take care, kid," Frank says and then hangs up.

UNCLE JAKE

My mom invites me over for dinner. She's making spaghetti and meatballs. Nobody can make spaghetti sauce like my mom, nobody. She used to try to make her own meatballs, but they'd always fall apart and tasted too oniony. My brother Bill and I would complain. She'd try to fake us out and tell us the meatballs she was serving were a frozen store brand, a kind we'd had and she knew my brother and I liked, but we always knew better and would call her out on it. I never understood why she tried to fool us. I mean, we knew she wasn't serving us store bought meatballs, we watched her make them. It always bothered me when mom lied to us. Our dad, on the other hand, never complained about anything our mom made. He'd gobble up whatever she put in front of him. After she gave up on trying to trick my brother and I with the meatballs, she started buying Purity, our local grocery store chain's frozen brand, and Bill and I quit complaining.

By the time I arrive, the sun's starting to go down. My uncle Jake's pickup is in the driveway next to my mom's car, so I park on the street. My mother has two brothers, one older and one younger. Jake is my mom's older brother. He lives a couple towns away. Jake's a lifelong bachelor. He dates, but he never seems to be able to find the right woman. Uncle Jake was a troublemaker as a younger man. He went to jail a couple times for robbery, though he was never away for too long. I love listening to him tell stories of his wild years.

Before I even open the screen door, I smell garlic bread. Jake is waiting on the deck with a bottle of beer in each hand. I haven't seen him in about three months. He's grown a beard and put on a considerable amount of weight. His facial hair is completely gray. He smiles so big I can see the space where a tooth used to be on the right side of his mouth.

"Long time no see, nephew!" He says as he hands me a beer. "This one's on me."

I smile and hold the bottle up. We tap our beers together as we walk inside the house.

"Where's mom?" I ask.

"Next door. She wanted to bring her boyfriend some of her famous homemade sauce."

"Boyfriend?"

"Well, she wouldn't call him that, but I don't know what else you'd call him," Jake says before taking a gulp from the bottle.

Curious, I pull the thick, beige curtain back and look out the window. I try to remember who my mom's neighbors are. The only single man in my mother's neighborhood that I can think of is two houses away, and he's my age and has two kids.

"Is it the Cutler house?" I ask.

"It's the fella in the green house diagonally across from here," Jake says, pointing over my shoulder.

"Don't point!" I yell. "I don't want them to know I'm looking," I pull the curtains shut. "Can't be. That's Craig Tapper's place. He's married."

"Nah, he's a widower," Jake says.

"Since when?"

"I guess his wife passed a month and a half ago."

"No shit?"

"Yeah, your mom wouldn't date a guy as young as Paul Cutler."

"How old's Craig Tapper?"

"Old enough," Jake says before burping loudly.

"How do you know all this?"

"Your mom and I talk on the phone pretty regularly."

"I had no idea."

The screen door opens, and my mom comes in. She's wearing a white apron with a blue flower pattern over a maroon sweatshirt and jeans. "Jesse!" she says, giving me a hug and kiss on the cheek.

"Hey, mom."

"You never told Jesse about your boyfriend?" Jake asks.

Mom looks at Jake and then at me and then begins to untie her apron. "He's not my boyfriend," she says, giggling while taking the apron off over her head.

"Well, what would you call him?" Jake asks, sitting down at the kitchen table.

"I don't know!" she says, blushing. "Who's ready to eat?" she says, changing the subject.

"I am!" I say.

"Well, I'm not waiting on either of you. You both know where the plates are. Have at it!"

Mom takes the garlic bread out of the oven, and the smell of the kitchen is immediately made ten times more delicious. I fill a plate with spaghetti and use a ladle to heap tomato sauce and Purity brand meatballs over it. I finish the plate off with a large piece of garlic bread on top of it all.

"You remember that time I took down that tree with Jared's moped?" Jake asks my mom.

"How could I forget?" my mother says, shaking her head.

"What?" I ask.

"Your uncle was trying to impress a girl."

"Stacy Fine," Jake says, smiling as he takes a big bite out of a piece of garlic bread. "You should've seen this girl, Jesse," Jake says through a mouth full of garlic bread. He sits back in his chair and chews the bread as he looks at the light fixture above the table longingly.

"Pretty?" I ask.

"Oh, boy," Jake says, making wavy motions with his hands in the air. "Curves!"

"She was fat," my mother says flatly.

"She was curvy," Jake says.

"Fat," my mom says adamantly.

"*Curvy,*" Jake insists, looking at me.

My mother looks down at her plate and shakes her head. "Fat," she whispers.

"Okay, so what happened with the tree and the moped?" I ask.

"Well, Stacy's old man had this dying tree in his yard, see? And if there was anything anybody in our neighborhood knew about Old Man Wise, it's that he hated that damn tree and couldn't wait to have someone take it down. Problem was, Mister Wise had two bad knees from his high school football days and could barely get around without a cane, so there was no way he was going to take it down himself. And, on top of that, he was dirt cheap. Too cheap to pay a service to come out and do it. The Wise family had no sons, just Stacy and her older sister, June, who was already grown and moved out, so I saw getting rid of that tree as an opportunity to get on Old Man Wise's good side.

"So, one day, there I was in the Wise driveway, talking Stacy up, testing the waters, hinting at maybe taking her to a movie, and she's telling me how her dad won't let her date. It was at that moment that I get this idea in my head that if I can take down that pain in the ass tree, maybe her dad will see me as a cut above all the other boys in the neighborhood, no pun intended, who want to take out his daughter, and he'll loosen up the reigns on his dating policy."

"Where does the moped fit into this story?" I ask.

"Well, that's where my pal, Jared Diamond, comes in," Jake says. "You see, Jared had this moped. He was the only kid in the neighborhood with motorized transportation and everyone always wanted to borrow it. But Jared was my best pal, and he wouldn't let anyone use it except for me."

"How old were you guys?" I ask.

"It was before we were old enough to get our licenses, maybe fourteen or fifteen."

"How did you date if you didn't have your license?"

"Somebody's mom or dad would drive us to the mall. Back in those days, the mall had a movie theater. So," Jake says.

"So," I say.

"So, I get this genius plan where if I take some rope and tie it around the highest part of the dying tree's trunk and attach the other end of the rope to the moped, I'm thinking I can pull the tree down and be a hero to Mister Wise and just maybe, *maybe* he'll ease up on his strict no-dating rule for yours truly and let me take his daughter to the mall to see a flick.

"First off, getting the rope up the tree was hard, because the damn thing was so dry, the branches kept breaking as I climbed. As soon as I found a good knot in the wood, I tied the rope tightly just below it, then I shimmied down and tied the other end of the rope below the moped's seat.

"So, I start the moped and try to get a running start, which was my first mistake. As soon as I drive the moped across the lawn and it reaches the end of the rope, the tree doesn't budge and the moped gets jerked backward. I go flying over the handlebars and somersault onto the lawn. I get up, and fortunately I'm not hurt too badly, but I really should have known better. I could have been killed."

"Were you wearing a helmet?" I ask.

"No helmet!" Jake says.

"You're lucky you didn't crack your skull open," I say.

"You should've given up at that point," my mother says, shaking her head.

"I wasn't giving up," Jake says. "So then, instead of getting a running start, I slowly drive the rope out to its full length and kick the moped into high gear. I look down, and the thing's rear tire is ruining the lawn, but I just thought to myself, 'I'll fix that when I'm done.' I was so determined, plus, Stacy was watching, and I wasn't going to embarrass myself twice. So, I'm flooring it, and the moped's engine starts smoking something wicked. Finally, the tree begins to give. I look over my shoulder and see it shaking and bending toward me.

"At long last, I hear the loud, satisfying cracking of dead wood. The moped rolls forward, and the next thing I know, the falling tree lands on top of Stacy Wise's mother's new car, destroying the hood and smashing the windshield."

"Oh no!" I say, laughing.

"Oh yes!" my mother says.

"So, I take it that was the end of you courting Stacy Wise?" I ask.

"Yes, it was," Jake says. "Fortunately, her mother had insurance to cover the cost of the damage the fallen tree had caused, but I still had to landscape the Wise's lawn and pay for repairs to the damage caused to my pal Jared's moped. Basically, every dime I made that summer mowing lawns and walking dogs went to fixing that dumb bike." Jake shakes his head. "And all to impress a curvy girl."

"Fat," my mother says without missing a beat.

"Did you ever get to take Stacy Wise out?" I ask.

Jake sighs. "I did, but it wasn't until we were both out of high school."

After dinner, Jake and I do the dishes while mom has a glass of wine in front of the TV. After Jake and I are done, we step outside for a cigarette.

"How you been, Jesse?" he asks.

"Been worse," I say.

"You workin'?"

"I'm workin'."

"I know what your brother was into, Jesse. If you're up to the same shady shit he was, you best be careful."

"I'm workin', Uncle Jake."

"Does your mom know what you're into?"

"She knows I'm traveling, but she thinks these jobs are all on the up and up."

Jake takes a drag off his cigarette and blows a cloud of smoke skyward. He seems lost in thought for a moment, as if there's something he's conflicted about telling me. I look over at him, and he looks at me sideways.

"You carrying anything heavy?" Jake asks.

"What, like a gun?"

"That's not what I mean."

"I'm not sure what you're talking about."

"I'm talking about your conscience, Jesse."

Jake looks out into the yard, and we're both quiet for a long moment.

"I sleep okay," I say.

"You know how Bill died?"

"The accident?"

"Accident," Jake says, shaking his head. He rolls his lit cigarette slowly between his thumb and forefinger, staring at it.

"What exactly are you implying?"

"You know your brother was coming back from a job that day he crashed?"

"Yeah," I say.

"Okay," Jake says, standing up and walking into the front yard, away from the porchlight.

For a moment, all I can see is the orange ember at the end of his butt. I stand and follow the glow into the darkness of the night.

"Are you trying to say Bill was murdered?

70

"That's not what I'm saying," Jake says into the dark. "I'm saying sometimes people get greedy and fate takes over. Sometimes folks don't know when to walk away from the table."

I lift my foot and put my cigarette out on the bottom of my sneaker. I walk back to the porch and toss the butt into a trash can. Inside the house, I say goodbye to my mother. She's already filled a Tupperware container with spaghetti and meatballs. I put it in my backpack and give her a kiss on the cheek before leaving.

As I descend the porch stairs, the screen door hits the frame, slamming shut behind me. From out in the yard, I hear Jake say, "Take care, Jesse."

2 DYE 4

I check the calendar on the wall of my bedroom. I have an appointment with my hair stylist this afternoon. The same woman has done my hair since I was in high school. Her name's Deb, and she runs a small operation out of the downstairs part of her house. Her shop is called 2 Dye 4. For the longest time, it was just Deb and one chair and one sink.

My mother's been friends with Deb for years. They went to high school together. Mom's always believed in supporting small businesses in town run by folks who graduated from her alma mater.

I shower but don't bother washing my hair, as I know Deb's going to wash it anyway. With a towel around my waist, I brush my teeth.

I open my bedroom window, light a cigarette, and turn on the stereo receiver. The local college station is playing a mix of popular and underground old school hip hop. It's sunny out, and the air isn't too cold. I dress in jeans and a gray t-shirt with a faux-vintage Pepsi logo on the front. I don't bother combing my hair. I grab my backpack from the back of the bedroom door and walk down the hall and into the kitchen.

"Morning, I made coffee if you're interested," Ben says, motioning to the pot with a clean plate as he empties the dishwasher.

"Thanks," I say as I take a travel mug out of the open dishwasher and find a top to fit it in the cabinet. I fill the mug with hot coffee, add a splash of half and half, and put the top on tightly. I take my helmet off the refrigerator and walk downstairs, sipping the coffee.

I get to 2 Dye 4 about ten minutes before my appointment. Deb's operation now consists of two chairs and two sinks. Inside, I take off my helmet and backpack and wave hello to Deb who's finishing up with a client. Deb's only other employee is a man who looks to be in his mid-forties. He has a moustache and thick, beautifully coiffed, longish brown hair. He's wearing a green, long-sleeve turtleneck straight out of an LL Bean catalog from 1987.

I sit in one of the waiting room chairs and slide the magazines on the coffee table around before finding a copy of

Rolling Stone. It's been a while since I flipped through an issue, and the magazine has fewer pages than I remember. There's a photo collage on the cover of celebrities. The front of the issue boasts The 100 Best TV Shows of All Time. I open it, expecting to find The Cosby Show ranked somewhere in the top ten. Strangely, I don't see it. I keep flipping pages, looking at every show and its ranking, and I realize The Cosby Show is nowhere to be found on Rolling Stone's list of the top one hundred TV shows of all time.

Growing up, there weren't too many shows Bill and I could agree on. When a Cosby rerun was airing, however, it pretty much guaranteed our parents thirty minutes of peace.

"Hey, Deb," I shout.

"What's up, honey?" she says, turning the hair dryer off.

"Have you looked at this Rolling Stone with the one hundred greatest TV shows yet?"

"No, baby," Deb says. "I haven't had a chance to look at it, why?"

"What would you say your top three favorite TV shows would be?"

Deb drops the hair dryer into an open drawer. "Hmmm…," She says as she takes the smock off her client and shakes it out.

"Seinfeld would be on there." Deb pauses. "Of all time?"

"Yeah," I say.

"So, it doesn't matter if it's still on the air?"

"Correct."

"In that case…I guess I'd say Seinfeld. I'd put Friends in my top three…and Cosby."

"I don't know if I'd put Cosby in my top three, but it would definitely be in my top five," I say. "Would you believe The Cosby Show isn't included anywhere on this list?"

"Nowhere?" Deb says.

"Nowhere on the list at all," I say, flipping through the pages as if to demonstrate that I searched the magazine thoroughly and couldn't find it.

"Why wouldn't they put Cosby on the list?" Deb says.

"Probably because of the rape allegations," Deb's male employee says as he rinses a customer's hair.

"Oh!" Deb says.

"But, still," I say. "I mean, a lot of other people helped to make that show great. And that show *was* great. I mean, it was on the air for a long time, right?"

"Yeah, it was great, but I'm sure the people who allege they've been hurt by Bill Cosby wouldn't appreciate seeing his face on their TVs, let alone his name on a list of the top one hundred TV shows of all time," the male hair stylist says.

"But, like, didn't the president admit to sexually assaulting women? Wasn't he caught on tape admitting to sexually assaulting women? Didn't, like, eleven women come forward and say they'd been sexually assaulted by him?"

"Seventeen women. Yeah, that happened," Deb says.

"So, why is it that Bill Cosby's show isn't included on this list, and yet Cosby has had all his awards and honorary degrees and whatnot taken from him, and his legacy is forever garbage, and all his work probably won't see the light of day for another hundred and fifty years, long after he's dead, when someone happens across it and believes it's safe to watch him again because Cosby and all his accusers have died and nobody's around to be offended by his face on their TV or whatever people are watching shows on in the future, and yet, another guy, who openly admits, actually *brags* about sexually assaulting women, and has accusers come forward and say they've been sexually assaulted by him...why is it okay for that guy to be elected to the highest office?"

"Because we live in a fucked up, backwards, racist country, that's why!" the woman Deb's just finished styling says as she steps out of the chair.

Everybody laughs but me.

Deb drapes the smock over the chair, walks over to the desk in the waiting area, and sits down behind it. The woman pays Deb and makes another appointment.

"Have a nice day," she says to me as she walks out the front door.

"Bye," I say.

"You ready, Jesse?" Deb asks.

"Yeah," I say as I stand and walk toward Deb with the Rolling Stone in my hand.

"Why don't you leave that on the table, honey," she suggests.

74

When I get back to the apartment, I find a letter in the mailbox addressed to me. I put the rest of the mail, which is all addressed to Ben, on the kitchen table, walk into my bedroom, and shut the door. I turn on the stereo. Weird, minimalist jazz drifts from the speakers.

I lie back on the bed and look at the envelope. My name has been printed onto a sticker and applied to the front of it. There's no return address. I know the letter is from Frank, because this is how he always sends the details of the jobs he hires guys for. I open the envelope and slide out a single white sheet of paper. Included on the sheet, in small print, in the very center of the page, are a starting date and time and an ending date. Below the dates and times are the name of the motel and the address.

I get off the bed and draw small diamonds in the boxes that correspond with the dates on the calendar as well as the time I need to be there. Zippo in hand, I walk into the bathroom. I turn on the ceiling fan and open the window. I set the sheet of paper on fire and use it to light a cigarette before dropping it in the sink. I sit on top of the toilet's tank with my feet on the closed lid, watching the paper burn.

"Hello?" a female voice says.

"Dawn?" I ask.

"Yes, is this Jesse?"

"Yes," I say.

"Hi," she says. "It's good to hear your voice."

"It's good to hear your voice. I missed it."

"Aw, that's sweet."

"I, uh, called because I'm going to be staying at that same motel where we met, and I wanted to see if maybe you'd like to meet up and get coffee or something?"

"Oh, just coffee?" she says sarcastically.

"Yeah, coffee and maybe a swim in the pool or a dip in the Jacuzzi. Listen, I'm not trying to twist your arm here or anything. I understand you're your own person, and I'm not looking to imply I'm going to show up expecting anything more than what we shared when I first met you."

Dawn laughs. "Listen to you! So precarious. You never considered I might be interested in more than just coffee?"

I feel my face getting hot. "Yeah, okay…I was trying to be a gentleman," I say, running my hand through my newly styled hair.

"You think that's what women want?"

"What, a gentleman?"

"Yeah."

My mouth dries up, and I can feel my face and neck getting warm. "Well…," I start.

"Well?"

I swallow.

"Hey," she says. "We're adults, Jesse. You don't have to be coy and play around anymore. That shit may have been cute in high school, but you're not the first guy who was interested in getting together for a fun night that included more than coffee and a swim."

"Okay," I say, realizing I have now lost complete control of the conversation.

"The next time you call a woman and ask her to meet up with you at a motel, maybe be more honest about what you want."

There's a long silence between us.

Ben walks into the kitchen, pours a cup of cold coffee into the sink, and puts it in the dishwasher.

"Is that a no?" I ask.

Dawn sighs. "I'll tell you what, Jesse; why don't you try again?"

"What, now?"

"Call me tomorrow, and when you do, drop the gentleman bullshit." Dawn hangs up.

I'm stunned. Ben is looking at me. I realize I'm no longer talking to anyone on the other end of the line, but I don't want Ben to know.

"Okay, I'll talk to you tomorrow. Bye," I say and hang up as soon as I pull the receiver away from my ear.

"You all right?" he asks, looking at me as he leans against the sink with his arms crossed over his chest.

"Yeah, why?" I ask as I shake a cigarette out and pull it from the pack with my lips.

"You look a little…flustered," he says.

"You ever get called out by a girl for being too nice?" I ask.

Ben laughs, shaking his head. "Yeah, once or twice, man," he says rubbing his eyes with his thumb and pointer finger.

"It's, like, my whole life I've been taught to be a gentleman and not to force myself on girls or imply I'm expecting something in exchange for anything and whatnot. Now, I'm a man, and I'm still trying to be a gentleman, and I'm getting flack for it. Do women think it's easy?"

"Think what's easy?" Ben asks, clearing his throat.

"You know, calling someone up and trying to arrange a get together."

"A get together? You mean asking someone out?"

I pause. "Yeah! Asking someone out," I say, sitting back in the chair and putting my hands behind my head.

"They know it's nerve wracking, man, but it's all part of the game."

"You think?"

"I know. Trust me. I mean, it's 2017, but women still want to be courted, you know?"

"Yeah, I guess. I mean, it's not like I've had a ton of offers in the other direction."

"You mean, women asking you out?" Ben asks.

"Yeah," I say, flicking my cigarette's ash in a cup on the table.

Ben reaches across the table for my pack of cigarettes. "May I?"

"Certainly," I say, pushing the pack and lighter toward him.

Ben lights a cigarette, pulls out one of the kitchen chairs, and sits down. He exhales a stream of smoke.

"If you're waiting for a woman to call you up and invite you over for sex, you're gonna be waiting a long time, my friend."

I laugh and look at Ben to see if he's joking. "That ever happen to you?"

He sighs. "In a roundabout sort of way, a couple times, yeah."

"What do you mean in a roundabout sort of way?"

"Like, I used to live in this single bedroom apartment downtown. There was this woman. We'd fuck. You know, just for fun.

"Anyway, it all started the first night I moved in. I was unpacking, and I had one lamp plugged into a long extension cord. I kept walking the lamp into other parts of the apartment to unpack, like, my toiletries and my clothes and my cutlery and dishes and stuff. I'm still unpacking at, like, eight or nine at night when the bulb blows. So now I need to either find another lamp or my lightbulbs or a flashlight, but for the moment, I'm in total darkness. All I can see is the light from the hall beneath my apartment's door.

"So, I go out into the hall and start knocking on doors, and the only neighbor who answers is a cute, short, biracial chick with a voluptuous figure. And she's, like, all put out that I need to borrow a flashlight. At this point, I'm thinking, why am I even bothering, you know? But she grudgingly gives me a flashlight, and I tell her thanks and that I'll bring it right back.

"So, I go back into my unit with her flashlight, and I'm looking through the boxes and trying to find the box with the stuff from my closet at my old place, because I know that's where I've

78

got, like, masking tape and, like, a measuring tape and glue and of course lightbulbs and a flashlight. You know, that kind of stuff.

"Anyway, I find the box and take out a pack of bulbs and walk back into the kitchen where the lamp with the blown bulb is. I replace the bulb and it doesn't work and I'm, like, 'Oh great, now what am I gonna do?' That's when there's a knock on my door.

"I open the door and it's completely dark in the hall. I'm, like, 'What the fuck?' and the biracial chick is standing there, and she says, 'Give me my flashlight back.'

"I say, 'What's going on?' She goes, 'What do you *think's* going on? We lost power, dickhead!' And I'm thinking to myself, what are the chances of this, you know?"

"You're making this up," I say, laughing and shaking my head."

"I swear to God, Jesse. This honestly happened."

"How did she know which apartment you were in?"

Ben pauses. "Good question. I guess she could see the light from the flashlight under the door."

"Okay, so then what happened?"

"Right, so then I'm, like, 'Can you just let me find my flashlight so I don't kill myself walking around in the dark?' And she's all, 'Hurry *up!*'"

Ben and I laugh.

"She says, 'I'm coming in.' And I'm, like, 'That's fine by me.' So, she's holding on to the back of my shirt, and I'm walking through my apartment with her flashlight, trying not to trip over any of the boxes all over the floor. I start digging through the box of stuff where the lightbulbs were, in hopes that there's a flashlight somewhere inside."

"What's she doing while you're doing that?" I ask.

"She's still holding onto my shirt and looking over my shoulder, and it's starting to bug me, because she's, like, pulling on my shirt really hard and the collar is cutting into my neck and finally I say, 'What the fuck is wrong with you?' Oh, and I forgot to mention, she won't shut up."

I start laughing so hard I begin to cough.

"Yeah, she won't shut up, and she's talking real fast about…nothing!"

"Like what? I gotta know what she's talking about."

Ben sighs and takes a drag off his cigarette and flicks the ash into the cup. "Like, I really wasn't listening, but it was just about, like, 'You know, this is just like the time the power went off during the storm we had last winter.' That kind of shit."

"Okay," I say.

"Okay, so, I'm trying to get her to back off on the shirt-pulling, and I grab her wrist and yank her hand off, and I realize she's gripping so hard because she's terrified of the dark."

"What?"

"Yup!"

"After all that tough talk?"

"Her hand was shaking with fear."

"Then what happened?"

"So, at the exact moment I grab her wrist and try to wrench her frightened fingers from my now completely ruined and stretched out shirt, a door in the hall outside closes and she jumps a mile. Like, 'Ahhh!' Now, mind you, we're both squatting on the floor, as I'm trying to look for my flashlight in this box. So, when the door in the hall closes, she jumps on me, like…you ever see the way a koala clings onto a person's leg with their arms and feet?"

"She was clinging like that?"

"Yeah, exactly like that. So of course I'm not ready for all that, and I fall back onto my butt and drop her flashlight and now neither of us can see a damn thing."

"And where is she at this point."

"Okay, I'm, like, on my back, right? And she's on top of me. I can feel her breath in my ear and on my neck."

"And you're being a gentleman."

"And I'm being a gentleman. That's how this whole conversation started, if I remember correctly," we both laugh. "Anyway, I'm being a gentleman and now I'm…"

"Was she a big girl?" I ask.

"Oh, you mean, like, was she fat?"

"Yeah. I mean, you said she was voluptuous…"

"No, I mean, she was curvy, but I wouldn't call her fat. I mean, she was proportioned, you know, considering her height and everything. I mean, probably even a little smaller than average.

Anyway, I'm trying to calm her down, and I'm being real patient and sweet, and I'm saying things like, 'It's okay. It's just a brownout. The power will come back on. I'm here. Where's the flashlight?' And she's just, like, 'I'm so embarrassed.' And I'm, like, 'There's no need to be embarrassed. Everybody's scared of something.'

"So, then she starts to ease up, and she thanks me for consoling her and everything, and we find the flashlight, and I stand up, and she stands up, and she gives me a hug for being nice and everything, and I hug her back, and I'm not thinking anything of it, and then she starts kissing my neck and, like, I don't know what to do. So, I just start kissing her neck, and she smells really good, and then she moves to my face and then we're making out and before I know it, we're taking off each other's clothes and she's on top of me and…"

"And where's the flashlight while this is going on?"

"The flashlight? Oh, the flashlight's on and it's, like, rolling around so we can sort of see each other, but mostly my hands were my eyes, you know what I'm saying?"

"Right, right," I say, smiling. "So, how did we get here again?" I ask, laughing.

"Okay, so, my point in telling you all this was to explain that this woman and I started fucking on the regular and it wasn't always me instigating it. Most of the time it would be, like, her calling me up and telling me her toaster was broken or some shit. I'd come over and her toaster wouldn't be broken at all. It would just be unplugged. I'd, like, plug in her toaster, then turn around and she'd be all over me within seconds."

"I hear you," I say.

Ben shakes his head. "It's the way of the world, man. It's just how we're made. I mean, you think there weren't shy cavemen? There had to be some cavewomen taking business into their own hands back in the day."

"How do you feel about a woman being more sexually aggressive than you?" I ask.

Ben shrugs. "I mean, It's not my preference. But beggars can't be choosers, you know?"

"So, how do I handle this when I call her back?"

"Man, just be direct. I mean, don't be graphic, but at least let her know your intentions without sounding filthy and creepy. You'll be all right."

"Okay," I say, nodding. "Thanks."

MACY'S

I'm going through the equipment in my duffel bag. I pull out all my drill bits and polish each one with a lightly oiled rag. I carefully inspect my tools, even the ones I've yet to use on a job. I take the drill completely apart and carefully clean each piece, making sure nothing's bent or dented. All it would take to get a crew pinched would be for my equipment to not function at one hundred percent, thereby causing a job to take longer than intended and increasing the risk of the authorities busting us.

I carefully put the drill back together and run it for about half a minute. Ben is out shopping with his bandmates downtown, and the drill isn't loud enough to be heard by the neighbors. As I'm finishing testing and inspecting my equipment and putting everything back in the bags, I look down and realize my shirt is filthy and torn. What's worse, the stains and holes in my clothes were there before I started to clean my equipment. I look at myself in the long mirror on the back of my bedroom door. I'm depressed by what I see.

I open my closet and carefully go through my shirts and pants one by one. Nothing looks new or nice. Everything's either wrinkled or worn down on the elbows and knees or frayed around the collar or stained from cooking oil or grease or something from my motorcycle. I definitely need new threads. I check my cash on hand, which I keep in a shoebox under the bed. I take a few hundred out of the envelope from the last job and push it into my wallet.

I empty my backpack and grab my helmet from the top of the refrigerator as I walk through the kitchen and downstairs. I get on my motorcycle and head toward the mall downtown. On my way, I try to remember the last time I bothered to update my wardrobe. It has to have been at least four years since I've done shopping that included anything more than new underwear or a pair of sneakers or socks.

I park my bike and walk into Macy's with my backpack over my shoulders, carrying my helmet. In the men's department, I find a few different shades of khaki dress pants in my size as well as a couple white dress shirts and a light blue one. I take everything into a dressing room and hang the clothes up on a hook. As I'm undressing, I hear what sounds like a mother and son just outside.

"I want to see each pair on you before I pay for any of this, Shawn," an annoyed older woman's voice says.

A male voice groans loudly. The door next to the dressing room I'm in shuts. "Whatever!" comes the response from what sounds like a teenage boy.

"Don't whatever me, Shawn. I swear, I'll leave right now without buying you anything. You can go to school naked for all I care."

"Shut up, mom!" Shawn says from inside the dressing room.

"Don't you tell me to shut up!" Shawn's mother says as she bangs on the door.

"Quit being a bitch!" the boy says.

"I'll quit being a bitch when you quit giving me attitude!"

I'm now standing stone-still in the dressing room with the jeans that I wore to the mall half on and half off. I'm amazed at the brazenness of the boy. I quietly step completely out of my dungarees and hang them on the wall opposite the clothes I'm trying on.

"Have you got any of those on yet?" the boy's mother asks, standing close to the door.

"Hang on!" Shawn says.

"What?" his mother says, even though I'm certain she heard him.

"I said, 'hang on!'" he yells.

The woman sighs. "Come on, Shawn. I don't want to be here all afternoon. I have to get home and make dinner."

The door opens, and through the wooden venetian-style slats on the lower part of my dressing room's door, I see Shawn's stockinged feet shuffle out. His socks are filthy and there's a hole in the heel of one of them. I watch as Shawn's mother's hands grip the cuffs of the pants the boy is wearing and begin to fold them upward. Her bracelets rattle as she yanks.

"Stand still!" she yells, tugging the leg of his pants down firmly.

"I am!" he whines.

"How do they fit in the waist area?" she asks.

"Fine," he says.

84

"They look tight."

"They're fine," he says.

"Let me see," she says.

Shawn huffs and I hear him pulling up his shirt.

"No, those are too tight."

"Can we just go?"

"Look at them," she says. I see a pair of black high-heeled shoes in front of the teen's dirty socks. "They look tight," Shawn's mom says again.

"They're fine!" Shawn says angrily.

"Come here," she says. The boy steps back. Shawn's mother stomps down hard with one foot and says, "Come *here*!" He sighs and moves forward.

"Look at this! I can barely get two fingers inside of the waistband. You can't wear these to school. At the rate you're eating these days, you're going to outgrow these in the next three months. Get back in that dressing room and try on another pair," the teen's mother says.

Shawn huffs. His feet turn and disappear. I hear a door close. I don't want to miss a minute of the arguing, so as Shawn is getting changed into a new pair of pants, so do I.

"Let's go, Shawn! I don't have all night!" his mother yells.

I hear the dressing room door open, and I see Shawn's gross socks again. This time the cuff of the pants he's trying on aren't long enough to reach the bottom of his feet.

"How do they feel?" his mother asks.

"Fine," he says.

"Pull up your shirt," she says. "Let me see how many fingers I can get in there."

I see the cuffs of the slacks Shawn's wearing jostle around, up and down and side to side. I wince, as I know his mother is putting this poor pair of pants through some sort of weird mom test.

"Can we go now?" he asks.

She kneels in front of her son, and I see her hands around the cuffs of his slacks. Her nylon covered knees are on the ground. A black skirt covers her calves and her upper thighs as she pulls at the pants her son is wearing.

"No! Nope! No good. These are no good," she says, sighing and slapping her hands on her thighs as she gets back up on her feet.

"Why?" Shawn whines.

"Look how short they are."

"They're not short."

"Sit down over there," she says.

I see the boy's feet move toward a chair, and then I'm unable to see anything else. I take off my t-shirt and try on one of the white button-down shirts I've brought into the dressing room. I pull the pins out and put them in a small pile on the bench next to my helmet. There seem to be an endless number of pins holding the shirt in its package.

"Look at how high these cuffs go up when you sit! No, these are no good," Shawn's mother says. "Get in that dressing room and try on another pair."

"But, mom!"

"Don't but mom me! Get in there and try on another pair! Now! We're not leaving until we find a pair that fits."

I'm trapped. That's all there is to it. This is why I haven't updated my wardrobe in a half decade. This is why I avoid department stores at all costs. There's no way I'm walking out of this dressing room with all this drama going on right outside. I'm here for the duration. I'm here until this whiny teen and his obstinate mother find a pair of friggin' pants that fit.

The door of the dressing room next to the one I'm in opens and out steps Shawn.

"Come here," his mother says quietly.

Shawn shuffles his feet a little but barely moves in the direction of his mother.

"For the last time, Shawn. Come! *Here*!" She yells.

I hear Shawn whimper exhaustedly and step quickly toward his mother.

Shawn's mother gets down on her knees again, yanking on the pants as she adjusts the cuffs, which, from where I'm standing, look just about right.

"Go sit down in that chair…again," she says tiredly.

Shawn's feet disappear from view, and I hear his mother sigh as she gets back on her feet.

There's a long moment of silence. "Okay," Shawn's mother finally says. "Get your jeans back on. We're buying those and getting the hell out of this store."

I sit down on the tiny wooden bench, wearing the dress shirt and khaki pants, rubbing my face with both hands, waiting patiently for Shawn to get dressed and for he and his mom to leave so I can finish what I came here to do without feeling self-conscious about listening to their conversation.

Only once do I remember my mother ever taking me to try on clothes at a department store. She was buying me a suit for her friend's wedding where I was to be the ring bearer. Otherwise, I'm pretty sure my mom couldn't be bothered hanging around in a department store, waiting for me to try clothes on, trying to decide if they fit or not. Now that I think back on it, she must have bought me clothes by eyeballing them, then bringing them home. If they fit, I'd wear them, and if they didn't, they went back to the store the next day.

Finally, Shawn and his mother leave. I try on the rest of the shirts and pants and decide to buy everything. I carefully pick up all the pins I'd taken out of the shirts and drop them into a small bucket near the entrance of the dressing room area.

I pay for my clothes and stuff the big Macy's bag into my backpack. I think about having to call Dawn again, and I'm remembering Ben's story and wondering if I have it in me to be direct without being creepy. On my ride back to the apartment, I begin to rehearse lines in my head that might sound both sincere and straightforward. Nothing feels right.

"Ah shit! Why am I even bothering?" I say out loud to the inside of my helmet.

PHONING DAWN

I'm looking at the calendar on my bedroom wall and trying to decide the best course of action regarding meeting up with Dawn. I know the room Frank has reserved is only good for one night. The plan is to hit the jewelry store and get the fuck out of Dodge immediately after.

Before I call Dawn, I contact the motel and tell the clerk I'd like to reserve the same room that's already in my name for the night before as well. The clerk confirms that it won't be a problem to hold the room for the night prior in addition to the night already booked. I inform her I'll be paying for the additional night separately when I arrive.

After the motel room arrangements are made, I smoke a cigarette and make myself a gin and tonic. I down the liquid courage, extinguish the butt, and pick up the phone. Ben is downtown at a cocktail lounge, getting ready to perform with his trio. I've got the house to myself, but I've also got no Ben to coach me before I make the call and nobody to make me feel better if I blow it. I pick up the phone and dial Dawn's number. The phone rings twice before she answers.

"Hello?"

"Hello," I say.

"Jesse," she says knowingly.

"How was your day?" I ask.

"It was okay."

"Tell me about it."

"Well, I worked. That means I was up and at the store before we opened to prepare the merchandise and make sure everything was presentable. Then I had to forego any breaks because one of my employees called in sick, so I was starving by the time I left to come home, and now I'm pigging out on leftover KFC and orange soda. How about you?"

"I did my usual stuff, showered, ate, smoked, and listened to the radio."

"Sounds like a pretty sweet day if you ask me, except for the smoking," Dawn says.

I decide now is as good a time as any to invite her to get together again at the motel where we'd first met. I screw up my courage and plow ahead.

"I want to see you again," I say.

"Okay," she says.

"I've reserved a room at the same motel where we first met."

"You have?"

"That's right," I say. "I want to meet you at that motel again, and I want to show you a good time."

"You do?"

"Yes."

At this point, I desperately want to say, 'Listen, I'm doing the best I can here! This is not at all the kind of person I am! Will you please just give me a break and tell me whether or not you'll be there so we can forego this charade?' But I don't say this. Instead, I keep going.

"I'm picking up the tab for everything," I say.

"You are?"

"Yes."

"And what about my room. Are you picking up the cost of my room?" she asks.

I pause, swallow hard, and say, "There's no *your* room."

"Really? Isn't that a bit presumptuous of you, Jesse?"

"No."

"No?"

"No."

"And why is that?"

"Because the room I reserved has two full size beds," I say.

Dawn laughs. I take this as a good sign and decide to close the deal.

"So, what do you say?" I ask.

There's a pause that feels like an eternity.

"I would love to see you again at the motel where we first met," she says at last.

I feel my lips turn into a smile. I give her the date and tell her to bring her bathing suit as well as something nice, because I plan on taking her out to dinner.

"I'll be driving there after work. I don't know exactly what time I'll arrive, but I'll be there before eight," she says.

"Okay," I say. "I'll make dinner reservations for nine."

"What room will you be in?"

"Two twenty," I say.

"I'll call your room when I get there," she says.

"Sounds great," I say, now thoroughly excited but doing my best to sound cool.

"Looking forward to it."

"Goodnight, Dawn."

"Goodnight, Jesse."

The next morning, I tell Ben about the phone call. He's impressed. Ben knows the area and recommends a nice restaurant nearby. I call the place and make dinner reservations for nine.

It's a beautiful spring day, sunny and not too hot. I decide to ride my motorcycle to the beach. Even though it's warm, I still wear jeans and a leather jacket for my trip to the coast. I've heard too many stories of guys wiping out on their bikes while wearing only shorts and a t-shirt, and sometimes not even that.

I leave well after everyone's gone to their day job so I don't hit any traffic. I make good time getting to the beach. I find a changing area with lockers just off the parking lot. I get into my swim trunks and flip-flops and put my socks, sneakers, jeans, helmet, and jacket into a locker.

I walk along the ocean's edge, occasionally wetting my feet in the sea. The water's freezing, but the waves are intermittent so it doesn't bother me too badly. Seagulls are everywhere, looking for scraps in the sand. It's windy and somewhat cooler at the ocean than it was when I left the house. Not exactly a good day for sitting outside in a bathing suit. I see only a couple kites and a few scattered sun umbrellas.

I leave the sand and cross the street, walking along the boardwalk. I stop and get a beef taco and a Coke from a truck and ask the young vendor where I can get a decent tattoo. He tells me the best place is American Ink, it's about two blocks down on the opposite side of the street. He says to ask for a guy named Rudy who

90

will do an excellent job at a fair price. The kid lifts the sleeve of his yellow t-shirt and shows me a tribal pattern on his bicep. He says Rudy was the guy who gave it to him. The art looks decent enough. I thank the kid and put a ten-dollar bill in his tip jar.

I have one tattoo on my body. It's a yin and yang symbol on my left shoulder. My uncle Jake took me to get it on my eighteenth birthday. I've been wanting to get a tattoo on my opposite shoulder for a while.

I finish the taco and soda just as I'm walking into American Ink. The place is small. Inside there's a woman working on a guy's back. She's giving the guy a tattoo of a bald eagle with its wings spread. Its claws are clutching arrows and an American flag.

"I'm looking for Rudy," I say.

"Yeah, he's out back," the woman says. "Rudy!" she yells.

A short, bald guy with a black moustache steps out from behind a curtain. He's wearing a black tank-top and jean shorts. Rudy's arms are covered in tattoos.

"What's up?" Rudy says as he approaches from the back of the parlor.

"I'm looking to get some ink today," I say.

"What are you thinking about?" he asks.

"I want a combination lock."

"Like a locker lock?"

"Yeah, not the whole locker. I only want the knob with the digits," I say.

"Okay," Rudy says. "Where do you want me to put it?"

"I want it right here," I say, pointing to my shoulder. "I want it roughly the same size as this yin and yang symbol I have," I say as I pull up the sleeve of my t-shirt.

Rudy looks at my yin and yang symbol. "That's not bad work," he says. "Did you get it in the city?

"Yes," I say.

"Can I guess where you got it?"

"You can guess, but I'm not going to remember. I got it when I turned eighteen."

"This looks like the work of either Jim Cantolone or Bob Sugarman," Rudy says.

"Could've been either or neither," I say. "I don't remember."

"Okay, well why don't you step into my office and we'll get this rodeo underway," he says.

I follow him into the back part of the parlor and take a seat at a table. On a laptop, Rudy shows me a variety of tattoo patterns for combination locks. I pick one that looks exactly like a Mosler. He prints the image out on contact paper and applies it to my arm. He takes his time, tracing the piece out with his needle. He works tirelessly, taking a break to sip from a cup of water once, and only after asking me if I want something to drink.

"You don't get to the beach too often, do you?" Rudy asks.

"How can you tell?"

"Well, you're definitely not a ray worshipper. I mean, your skin hasn't seen the sun in a long time."

I laugh. "Yeah, well, that's most definitely the case."

It takes Rudy about an hour and a half to complete the tattoo. He never asks me what the significance of a combination lock is. I pay him for the work and give him a generous gratuity. He takes a couple photos of the artwork to hang in the shop. I wonder who else on the planet would want a tattoo of a combination lock.

I go to an arcade on the boardwalk and play a couple dollars-worth of pinball on a few old machines. Afterward, I get an orange slush at a stand and walk back across the street until I'm at a bench under an awning. I sit down, light a cigarette, and watch people walking back and forth along the beach.

A young guy and girl stroll by with a dog. The couple throw a Frisbee ahead of themselves as they walk. Their dog gleefully runs after it, picks the disc up in its jaws, and brings it back to them. The couple and their dog appear to be happy.

After I've been at the beach for the better part of the afternoon, I look at my watch and decide that if I'm going to avoid any traffic caused by commuters, I'd better leave now. I go back to my locker and empty it.

My leather jacket's constant rubbing against my shoulder due to the vibration of the motorcycle's engine combined with the bumpy road, reminds me that my arm was under the sting of a tattoo needle just a couple hours earlier. But even though there's room in my backpack for my jacket, there's no way I'm risking riding all the way home without my torso completely covered.

On the way back from the beach, I stop at a McDonald's and pick up a Big Mac, Coke, and fries in the drive-thru. I eat everything in the parking lot, standing next to my bike. A couple teenaged boys come by on skateboards. One stops and asks how long I've had my motorcycle.

"Just over two years," I say.

"Can you do a wheelie?" the other boy asks.

I laugh. "I've never tried."

"How fast can it go?"

"I think it tops out at one twenty."

"Whoa!" they say simultaneously.

"Can I try it?" one of the teens asks.

I laugh again. "I don't think that would be legal."

"Why? I'm sixteen," the boy says.

"Are you licensed to drive a motorcycle?" I ask.

"Sure I am!" the kid says.

"No you're not!" his friend says, laughing.

The boy who wants to ride my bike punches his friend on the shoulder.

"Was it expensive?" the kid asks.

"The bike? It cost me about seven grand."

"What's your job?" one of the boys asks.

"This and that," I say, shrugging.

"Do you own a gun?" they ask.

"A gun? No," I say, laughing.

"If I had a bike like that, I'd own a gun," one of the boys says.

"Why would you need a gun?" the other boy asks.

"I don't know. In case anyone tried to steal my motorcycle, I guess," he says.

"My brother has a gun," the other boy says.

"He does not!" replies his pal.

"He does so!"

"No way he does!" the teen argues back.

"He does!"

93

"How do you know?" his friend asks.

"Because I found it once."

"Where?"

"It was in his closet in a paper bag."

"Why would he keep his gun in a paper bag?" his friend asks, laughing and looking at me as if to see whose side I'll take in the dumb argument.

"How the hell should I know? Probably as good a place as any to keep a gun," the kid says.

The two teen boys get bored with me and begin to skate around the parking lot. I throw out my cup, put my helmet on, and ride out of the lot.

When I get back into town, I drive to a place called Mike's Tavern, which I sometimes frequent. Inside, I take a stool at the bar and put my helmet underneath it.

"What'll it be, Jesse?" Mike, the bartender asks.

"Give me a Michelob."

Mike pops the top on a bottle and puts it in front of me. An older man with gray hair and a beard, wearing a plaid shirt and jeans, sits down next to me and puts a paper bag on the bar in front of him.

"You wouldn't happen to have a gun in there, would you?" I ask.

"Huh?" the old-timer says as he turns, an annoyed expression on his dry, wrinkled face.

"Nothing," I say, shaking my head.

"Hey, kid," the old guy says.

I look over. He picks up the paper bag and dumps it out on the bar. Batteries of all different shapes and sizes fall out and roll all over the place. The man laughs, wheezing and toothless.

"What'll it be, Albert?" Mike asks the guy.

"The usual," Albert says as he scrapes the batteries together and drops them into the paper bag one by one.

Mike brings Albert a Coors in a bottle and opens it in front of him, throwing the cap over his shoulder into a trash can.

"Cheers, kid," the old man says, holding the bottle up.

I hold my bottle up and take a swig. We're both quiet for a moment.

"I used to keep a pistol in a paper bag," the old man says. "We all did."

I turn in my stool and face the man. "Why would anyone keep a gun in a paper bag?" I ask.

Albert shrugs and takes another swig of his beer. "I guess it's like that saying, hiding in plain sight. You ever hear that saying?"

"Sure," I say.

He takes another sip of beer and burps. "If you were looking for a gun anywhere, why would you check a paper bag, you know what I mean?"

I nod. "I guess so, yeah."

I pick up my helmet, order another bottle of beer, and take it outside, standing in a roped-off area so I can smoke a cigarette while I drink.

"Used to be we could smoke inside," Albert says as he follows me, lighting a cigarette for himself. "After a hard day's work, you could go to a bar with your buddy and have a couple brews and smoke indoors during snow storms and whatnot. Not anymore," he says, exhaling a stream of smoke.

"What do you do?" I ask.

"Huh?"

"For work, I mean."

"I'm retired," he says as he launches into a coughing fit.

"What *did* you do?" I ask as soon as he stops hacking.

He shrugs. "Little of this, little of that." He looks at me sideways.

"Say no more," I say, smiling.

Albert winks and laughs, wheezing as he flashes a toothless smile.

When I get back to the apartment, I take a few Advil to ease the pain of the tattoo needle, then I lie down in bed and think about Dawn. I roll over and turn on the radio. A woman is singing lyrics about shots being fired on the street by the church where we used to meet. I fall asleep, listening to the sad words of the beautiful ballad.

I wake in the middle of the night and undress, being careful of my shoulder. I shut the stereo and the light off and go back to sleep.

LAST MINUTE ERRANDS

It's about a three-hour ride from the duplex to the motel. I can check in any time after eleven, but I've got a couple things to get done at home before I leave town. I borrow Ben's iron to smooth out my new shirts and pants.

"What's the occasion?" he asks.

"I'm going to take out that girl I was talking to you about."

"Yeah?"

"Yeah," I say.

Ben holds up his hand, and we high five.

"I'm gonna be gone for the next two days," I say.

"Right on," he says, sipping a cup of coffee.

In my room, I pack my new clothes neatly into a suitcase, including a bathing suit and dress shoes. I pull the shoebox full of cash out from under the bed and stuff my wallet full of hundreds.

When I'm done, I walk into the kitchen, light a cigarette, and make a fresh pot of coffee. I hear Ben's bandmates walking up the stairs. I open the door for them. As soon as they enter, carrying their equipment, Ben heads downstairs to help with the rest of their stuff. The trio moves the furniture in the living room to make space for the drums, keyboard, and amps.

I sit on the couch in the middle of the trio's jam session and sip my coffee. The group sounds better each time they play together. Instead of sounding like one long piece with short breaks in between, their songs are beginning to distinguish themselves in my untrained ears. The rehearsals usually begin with Ben providing a simple melody and he and his bandmates taking turns soloing over it.

After about an hour of relaxing, listening to Ben's trio, I decide to take a trip over to my mother's house to see if she needs anything done before I leave town. I call and make sure she's home before coming over.

"Mom, it's Jesse."

"What's up?"

"I'm going to be leaving town this afternoon for a couple nights. I was calling to see if you need anything done before I go."

"The lawn really needs to be cut," she says. "Normally I'd say it would be okay to wait until after you come back, but it's

96

supposed to rain all next week, and I'm afraid that if I wait until it's sunny again the grass will be too long."

"Okay, I'll come by and mow it today before I leave."

I change into a stained t-shirt, some old shorts, and a pair of beat up sneakers. I put money for rent and my share of the bills into an envelope. Ben and his bandmates are shooting the shit in the living room, taking a break from their music. I wave the envelope and whistle as I walk by. Ben gives me a thumbs-up.

"I'll leave it on the table," I say.

"Right on," he says.

When I get to my mom's house, I go right to the shed and pull out the lawnmower. I find the gas container dry and remember that I'd put it away empty the last time I cut the grass.

Other than the TV, I don't hear any noise coming from inside my mother's house. I try to open the screen door and find it locked, which is weird, because I never even knew the screen door had a lock. I ring the bell and hear heavy footsteps from another part of the house. Craig Tapper, my mother's new boyfriend, steps into view.

"Oh!" he says, sounding surprised to see me. He unlocks the screen door. "How's it going, Jesse?"

"Hey," I say, opening it. "It's going okay, thanks." I've only talked to Craig Tapper on a couple occasions in the past. Our conversations were brief and they all took place in the street while we were both shoveling snow. This was when I was living at home and Bill was still alive. "Sorry about your wife," I say.

"Thanks," he says. "You looking for your mom?"

"Yeah," I say.

"She's in the bathroom."

"Can you just let her know I went to get gas for the mower and that I'll be right back?" I ask, holding up the empty can.

"Sure thing," he says, smiling.

"I'm going to need her car keys," I say, taking my mother's keys off the kitchen table. I nod at Craig and walk back outside.

My mother is much smaller than I am. I push her seat back and readjust the mirrors so I can see behind me. As I drive to the gas station down the street, I play back my surprise at seeing Craig

Tapper come to the door. I wonder what he was doing at my mom's place in the middle of the afternoon and why she'd let him hang around when she knew I was coming over.

At the gas station, there's a guy scratching lottery tickets at the counter while the clerk, a round-faced, stocky, young woman with tattoos on both of her forearms and hair pulled back in a ponytail looks on. I reach into my back pocket and pull out my wallet.

The man stops scratching and sighs. "Son of a cunt!" he says, slapping the counter. He tosses the coin he was using to scratch the tickets into the take a penny, leave a penny bowl.

"Nothin'?" the clerk asks.

"Not a Goddamn thing!" he yells. "Fuck," he whispers as he turns and walks by me and out the door.

The clerk picks up the small stack of scratch tickets, rips them in half, and throws them in the trash beneath the counter. I step up, put down a ten, and give the woman my pump number.

Outside, I fill the gas can and carefully screw the cap on. I put it in the trunk of my mother's car and go back inside to collect my change from the cashier. She has it ready for me before I even ask.

I drive my mother's car back to her house. I'm dying for a cigarette, but I know better than to smoke in my mom's car. When I get back, I carefully remove the can and fill the lawnmower.

"Jesse!" my mom calls from the screen door.

I casually walk up to the front of the house, pushing the mower. I take a cigarette out and tap it on the pack. "What's up?" I say, putting the butt between my lips and pulling out my Zippo.

"Did you get gas?"

"Yep," I say as I light the cigarette and blow a stream of smoke from the side of my mouth.

"How much was it?"

"Less than twelve," I say. She turns to get her purse. "Mom," I say. She stops in the doorway. "Don't worry about it."

"Thanks," she says.

I consider mentioning Craig Tapper, but I don't, and I don't know why. I guess it's because I want my mom to be happy. Why shouldn't she have a special friend that she doesn't have to explain to anyone? After all she's been through, doesn't she deserve at least that?

After I cut the grass, I put the mower back in the shed and light a cigarette. My mom comes outside with an open bottle of Michelob and hands it to me. I nod and take a sip as I sit down on the stairs that lead to her deck.

"So, is this trip you're taking for work?" she asks.

I nod. "I'm also going to meet up with a friend."

"A woman?"

"Yes," I say before taking another sip of beer.

"Is it the same woman you'd met the other time you had to travel for work?"

"Yes."

My mother's quiet for a moment. "Well I think that's great."

"Thanks," I say.

I ride my motorcycle back to the duplex. After showering, I pack away all the toiletries for my trip, including my razor, shaving cream, toothbrush, dental floss, soap, and shampoo. I put everything into a shaving kit and put it in my suitcase. I call a taxi and wait outside with my bags.

I watch kids ride their bikes up and down the sidewalk. I try to remember being that young. I try to remember feeling free of responsibilities and enjoying time with friends, but I can't.

When I was younger, I spent a lot of time with my father and my brother. On the weekends, dad would take Bill and I to the high school and throw a football with us. We'd take turns running plays and giving them silly names, like the Liar, Liar Pants on Fire, and the Deep Creep. Two of us would be the quarterback and wide receiver, drawing out simple plays on the football, holding it between us. The receiver would hike the ball to the quarterback and then run out and try to fake out the man in the field who would try to either intercept the ball or bat it away before the receiver could catch it.

For me, the best times were when it was my brother Bill and I as the quarterback and receiver and my dad as the defense. Dad never let us win without putting up a fight. He'd always do his best to thwart the catch. It made my brother and I try that much harder.

After football, dad would take us out for subs and sodas. We'd get the food to go and then drive back to the field and eat the subs on the empty bleachers, laughing about the plays and the afternoon's memorable moments.

The taxi arrives. As soon as the driver sees I have a large duffel bag and a suitcase, he pops the trunk and offers to help.

"Thanks, but I can handle it," I say as I lift the bags and put them in the trunk of his old, red Volvo.

I sit in the passenger seat. The driver appears to be Hispanic. I'm sure he's older than me, but it's hard to tell by how much. He's wearing a plaid, long-sleeve shirt and blue jeans. He has short hair and a thin moustache.

"What's your name, man?" he asks.

"Jesse," I say. "What's yours?"

"Miguel."

"You know where we're going?"

Miguel laughs. "Yeah, man, I know where you're going."

"How long have you been doing the taxi thing?"

"About three months."

"Do you like it?"

"It's okay. It's not my full-time job, but it's a good way to earn some extra cash."

"What's your full-time job?"

"I have a cleaning service."

"Yeah?"

"Well, the business actually belongs to my brother and my sister and me. We clean offices after they close for the day."

"How long have you guys had that going?"

"About seven years now."

"Seven years? Business must be good."

"It's okay. We've got a few contracts. It makes for some long nights, but the money's decent, and it frees up our days to take care of our families and stuff."

"Do you like working with your siblings?"

Miguel laughs. "Sometimes."

"Only sometimes?"

"Yeah, I mean, sometimes we get into disagreements and then someone will want a night off or someone has to leave early and we have to figure out who gets paid what and how much if they weren't there the whole night. It can be a pain, because they're family and you can't fire them, you know?" We're both quiet for a moment. "You got any brothers and sisters?"

"I had a brother."

"Older or younger?"

"Older," I say. "He died in a car accident."

"That sucks."

Miguel takes an onramp onto the highway.

"You mind if I smoke?" I ask.

"Nah, just open the window."

I light a cigarette and roll down the window.

"You a smoker?" I ask.

"Used to be."

"What made you quit?"

"It was the only way my girlfriend would agree to move in with me. She said she'd never live with a smoker, because her dad died of lung cancer."

"Are you glad you stopped?"

"Yeah, I mean, it was three years ago that I quit, but I still miss it. I mean, I don't miss spending thirty bucks every week on cigarettes. I don't miss waking up, hacking every morning, and I don't miss feeling self-conscious about how I smell when I'm in an elevator or a car with a non-smoker. But I do miss having a cigarette first thing in the morning and with coffee or beer, and I miss smoking after a meal.

"I miss the ritual; you know? Like, I miss having a pack on my hip or in my breast pocket. I miss tapping the box before opening it. I miss pushing back the lid and flipping over cigarettes for the first letters of my girlfriend's first and last name for good luck. I miss shaking out a cigarette first thing in the morning. I miss tucking extra cash into the plastic wrapper around a hard pack, but, more than anything, I miss soft packs. I always felt like I was getting away with something when I had a soft pack of smokes. Old school, you know? Like, soft packs felt streamlined, and they were always a little cheaper price-wise, and I loved the accessibility. Like, with a soft pack you can customize the opening. I'd tear off a corner and shake butts out of it. It felt like a dispenser, you know? Like a gumball machine that drops the ball right into your hand rather than a snack machine with a big door you have to push to get your stuff out. I miss picking out a new lighter every few months, too." Miguel stops and looks over at me, as if to gauge my interest.

"Keep going," I say.

"Yeah?" he asks.

"Yeah."

"Because I got more!" he laughs.

"Say what you have to say. I'm just the passenger."

"Okay, let's see…I miss, like, the social aspect of smoking. I miss hanging out with other smokers and shooting the shit. I miss an excuse to step outside when things are getting boring or stressful. I miss loaning another smoker a cigarette and making a new friend. I miss leaning over, cupping my hand around a lighter's flame and lighting someone else's butt. I miss leaning into someone else's flame and nodding thank you. As weird as it may sound, I miss the sight of smoke leaving my mouth. I miss blowing it through my nostrils like a dragon. I miss flicking the ash off the end. I miss late nights, drinking with friends and seeing how long I can smoke a cigarette without the ash falling. I miss flicking a cigarette out of a car window and watching it spark and bounce with orange stars in the street behind my car.

"Shoot, that's almost poetry right there," I say, laughing. "What about ashtrays? Filthy things. You don't miss ashtrays, do you?"

"I *do* miss ashtrays, believe it or not," Miguel says, laughing. "I miss weirdly shaped ashtrays painted strange colors, and round, plastic ashtrays that look like castle turrets with those squared notches all around to hold your butt. I even miss cheap, tin, fast food restaurant ashtrays. Remember when you could smoke in McDonald's?"

"That was a little before my time," I say.

"Oh," Miguel says. "In the end, I guess I love my girlfriend, and I love my life, and I want to live, and I don't want to go out with a hole in my neck or some shit, and I'd rather not have a heart attack I knowingly paid for. I'd rather not have to have loved ones watch me suffer for months in a hospital bed connected to a machine that's breathing for me or something. Overall, I'm glad I quit, but I do miss it, yeah."

I throw my cigarette out the open window, put the seat back, and fall asleep. I dream I'm caught in a snowstorm. I'm wearing winter boots, a parka with a fur-lined hood, thick gloves, and snow pants. The snow's deep, and it's coming down hard all around me, though, other than the sound of the flakes gently falling on the hood of my parka, it's quiet. The landscape is hilly. I'm having a hard time walking, and the winter weather is so blinding that I can't make out the elevation, so I just keep my head down and concentrate on putting one foot in front of the other.

All at once, I lose my footing and begin somersaulting down an incline, coming to a stop after I roll into a tree. Fortunately, my parka is so thick I barely feel the impact. I stand and see that there's a hole in the tree's trunk. I reach inside and pull out a paper bag. I open the bag. Inside is an old revolver. This is when I wake up.

"You alright, bro'?" Miguel asks.

I rub my eyes, put the seat back up, and stretch. "Yeah," I say. I take a cigarette out and light it. I watch the signs on the highway. We're about ten minutes outside of the town where the motel is.

"You doing business out here?"

"Meeting a friend," I say.

Ten minutes later, Miguel is pulling into the motel parking lot. I pay him double the cost of the ride. He offers to help me with my luggage, but I tell him I can handle it on my own and ask him to pop the trunk.

I carry my duffel bag and suitcase into the lobby, placing them down on either side of myself as I stand at the counter, waiting for the clerk to notice. The woman working the desk looks at me and my bags suspiciously. For a moment, I'm worried.

"Did you stay with us a few weeks ago?" she asks.

"Yes, as a matter of fact I did," I say, doing my best not to appear nervous or concerned by her question.

"I thought so!" she says. "Welcome back."

"Thank you," I say, forcing a laugh.

I take my bags up to my room and lock the door. I put my suitcase on the bed and open it. I carefully remove the new clothes that I'll be wearing on my date and hang them up so they don't get wrinkled any more than they already are from being packed away. I pick up the room phone and call Dawn. Her voice mail picks up instantly. This time I remember to keep my message brief.

"Hey," I say. "It's Jesse. I'm at the motel. I'm in room two twenty. Give me a call when you get into town. See you soon."

It's still early. I'm guessing Dawn won't arrive for another couple of hours. I take my clothes off and bring my shaving kit and toiletries into the bathroom. After I shave and shower I do my best to replicate the hair style Deb gave me, even going so far as to use the motel room's hair dryer. When I'm done and somewhat satisfied with how I look, I fuck my hair up by pulling a white undershirt over my head. I don't bother trying to fix it.

I sit on the bed and turn on the TV. I stop changing channels when I see Norm Macdonald being interviewed. The host shows an old clip of Macdonald at a White House function during the Clinton administration. The joke Macdonald tells in the clip is about a recent injury the president incurred around that time, which caused Clinton a considerable amount of physical pain. Macdonald jokes that Bill's pain could be alleviated with the assistance of medical marijuana, which the president would have to inhale. The joke hasn't aged well and seems to stand as a testament to the stodginess of the nineties. After Macdonald's punchline, the president is shown laughing, his head back, his face red.

After the clip, Macdonald tells the host about his encounter with Bill Clinton. He first describes how big and red Bill's face was. He then talks about Hillary, saying how she appeared sour and miserable. He says the president went through the audience, greeting everyone in attendance. When he came around to Norm, he said something like, "Looks like you got a pickle there," referring to Norm's plate.

I change the channel and watch a black woman performing a song. She's wearing a gold dress and heels and is being backed by a seven-piece band that includes horns and bongo drums. I turn the volume on the TV up, then stand and open the sliding door that leads out to the deck. I light a cigarette and leave the door open so I can hear the music from the television. I stare at the abandoned office building across the street where I'm to meet Frank and Walt tomorrow night. The place appears dark and ominous.

In my room, I check my wallet and count my cash. I pick up my dress shoes, examining them in the light to make sure there aren't any scuff marks.

I turn the volume on the television down, lay back on the bed, and listen to the music. I've got a long night ahead of me. When the music program ends, I shut the TV off, pick up my wallet and room key, and walk downstairs, through the lobby, and outside.

I cross the street and enter the coffee shop. Inside, a young guy is cleaning the counter with a rag. There are only two other people in the shop. Both patrons are men who look like they're here for the same reason I am, killing time before a date. One man is dressed in hip, clean clothes, as if he's ready for a night out on the town. The other man is dressed conservatively, with a shirt and tie beneath a sweater vest. The man who's dressed more casually is sitting at a table by himself with a steaming cup of coffee. He holds a phone in front of his face and swipes at the screen with one finger while one of his knees bounces up and down nervously, his heel tapping audibly on the floor under the table.

The man with the tie and sweater vest sits at a table on the opposite side of the café, leaning over a book. Next to him is a pencil and a steaming cup of what I assume to be tea. Every now and again, the man sniffs before scratching a note into the margin of the pages, then adjusts his spectacles.

I walk up to the counter and order a small hot coffee. The kid pours me a cup and says, "One dollar." I pay for the coffee, stuff a five-dollar bill in the tip jar, and walk over to the cream and sugar station, adding a shot of cream, but also sugar to keep me alert for the next few hours. I take a seat at a table near the window and watch cars pass. I sip the coffee and try to imagine how things will go tonight. I wouldn't say I'm nervous, but I know I run the risk of destroying any spontaneity by overthinking things.

I turn my thoughts to the job I'm doing with Walt and Frank tomorrow. Something about the way Walt was talking the other day at breakfast has me wondering if he'll be involved in too many more crews Frank puts together. I'm thinking about how Walt sounded during our phone conversation the other night, and I'm wondering if he'll appear injured when I see him.

I know Walt's in need of cash, and I fear that he'll take any gig that comes his way. The fact that he's just come off a botched job leads me to wonder if he's wanted, and if he's wanted, if he is being followed by the feds, and if he's being followed by the feds, could he take Frank and I down with him? My mind continues down this dark, stressful path until I feel myself getting out of breath. I find myself tapping nervously on the table with my fingertips. Is this the heaviness my uncle warned me about?

"Hey," a female voice says.

I stop tapping and turn to see Dawn standing next to my table. She's wearing a bright blue dress that comes down to just above her knees, with white heels and a white leather purse over her shoulder.

"How did you know I was here?" I ask.

"I called your room. When you didn't answer, I figured there were only a couple places you could be."

I smile. "Are you ready to go?"

"I should be asking you that question," she says. "After all, I'm the one with the car, right?"

"That's true," I say as I stand. "It's good to see you. You look great."

We hug. Her arms wrap around my shoulders and neck. Her skin feels soft on mine. She smells sweet. I'm wishing I'd remembered to wear cologne.

"Did you come right from work?" I ask.

"I went home and showered and changed before leaving. Shall we?" she asks.

"One moment," I say. I finish what's left of my coffee and wipe my mouth with a napkin. "Let's do this."

"How was work?" I ask as we drive out of the motel parking lot.

"Work was work," she sighs. "I'd really rather not talk about it. How's work going for you?"

"I'd really rather not talk about it," I say.

"What did you do today?" she asks.

106

"I got this haircut."

"I like it."

"Thanks," I say. "I had a hard time recreating the look my stylist gave me."

"That's one of the reasons I've stayed with the same hairstyle for as long as I have. It's easy to just brush it straight and part it on the side. My hair's gotten trained over time, you know?"

"Oh, I also got a new tattoo," I say.

"I noticed you had a tattoo on your shoulder when we were at the pool. It's a yin and yang, right?"

"Yeah," I say.

"What's the new tattoo of?"

"It's a combination," I say.

"A combination? What do you mean, like, it's two different things?"

"No, it's a combination, like, on a lock, you know, with numbers…?"

"Oh! Okay, that's…different," she says. "What's the significance?"

"Well, locks are how I make a living, and I've always been into keys and tumblers and padlocks and safes. I thought I'd honor my occupation with a tattoo of a combination lock."

"Will you show me?"

"Maybe, if you're lucky," I say, smiling as I look out the passenger side window.

"Where'd you get the tattoo?"

"The beach."

"No, where on your body did you get the tattoo?" she says, laughing.

"Oh! It's on my other shoulder. Do you have any tattoos?" I ask.

"Maybe if you're lucky you'll find out," she says.

I feel my eyebrows jump. I glance over to see if she noticed. She's smiling, but her eyes are fixed on the road.

"What's this?" I say, touching a small wooden loop with feathers that's swinging from her rearview mirror.

"That's a dreamcatcher," she says. "You've never seen a dreamcatcher?"

I shake my head. "Kind of looks Native American."

"Yeah, that's exactly what it is," Dawn says. "It's to catch all the bad dreams while you sleep."

"Why is it in your car? Do you sleep in here or something?"

"Hey! I thought it was pretty, all right?"

As we drive, I give Dawn directions to the steakhouse I'd made our dinner reservations at. It's a place called Carlos' House of Beef. The parking lot is well-lit, and as we exit the car, music can be heard coming from speakers shaped like rocks in the beautifully manicured lawn surrounding the building. The pleasant melodies resemble something you might hear on an AM station late at night. Jazzy, but not inaccessible. I take Dawn's hand as we walk across the parking lot and up the ramp to the restaurant. Her fingers are thin and soft. She threads them through mine.

A man in a suit, standing outside the door of the restaurant says, "Good evening," and holds the door open for Dawn and me.

We step into a dark, wood paneled room with a thin rug. The smell of the lobby is clean and flowery. A hostess stands at a podium, her face illuminated by a tiny blue bulb attached to the end of a device that resembles a microphone. She's wearing a tight, black, sequined evening dress that goes over one shoulder. The hostess has thin gold hoop earrings and her auburn hair is arranged in a bun on top of her head. She appears to be attractive, but there's not enough light to really tell for sure.

"Welcome to Carlos'," the woman says. "What's the name?"

"Jesse," I say.

"Party of two?" she asks.

"Yes," I say.

"Right this way, please."

The hostess takes two menus off her podium and turns, walking into the darkness of the steak house. As soon as we're beyond the lobby area, the lighting becomes soft and romantic. A hue similar to the light on the hostess' podium seems to come from the underside of every table, causing all the patrons' faces to appear blue. It's just enough light so that the seated parties can see one another, but not enough to highlight imperfections or flaws in their hair or clothing.

The hostess seats us in a booth made up of one continuous curved leather seat. We slide in on opposite sides. I peek under the table to see where the blue light is emanating from.

Dawn scans the single page menu. Her face is even more beautiful in the light. She catches me staring. I smile. She smiles back. I look down at my menu. A woman comes to our table with a plate of bread and a pitcher of ice water. She carefully turns our glasses over and fills them. I nod at her. She smiles and then disappears into the darkness.

Our waiter comes to the table and introduces himself as Joel. He's wearing a black turtleneck that fits his trim frame snugly. His black hair stands straight up. From his apron, he pulls out a small, black notepad and a pen with a blue light at its tip.

I order a drink called a Purple Rose of Cairo. It's made with purple Hpnotiq liqueur, champagne, and Chambord. Dawn orders a drink called a Sunset Rubdown, made with Bombay Sapphire gin, coconut water, and frozen strawberries.

"Thank you for coming," I say to Dawn.

"I'll be honest, after that first phone conversation, I didn't know if you'd call back."

"You knew I liked you. You knew I wanted to get together. I'm not the kind of person who gives up so easily."

"I'm glad," Dawn says. She reaches out and touches my hand. I smile and turn it palm-up, holding hers. "I *was* kind of demanding, though," she says. "But I honestly don't want any games. I just want someone who's going to be honest about their intentions. We had fun when we first met and everything, and you seem like a genuine person, but I just felt like if this is going to work, I wanted you to come clean about some things."

"What things?" I ask.

"Like, what you're really doing here," Dawn says, suddenly serious. She takes a sip from her glass of ice water.

"I'm here to see you," I say.

She shakes her head and pulls her hand away from mine just as Joel brings our drinks. I can't tell if Dawn's pulled her hand away because the waiter has brought our drinks to the table or if she's suddenly not as interested in me because she suspects my reason for being here includes more than just our evening together.

"A toast," I say, lifting my glass. Dawn lifts hers. "To us."
We clink glasses and sip our beverages. "How's yours?" I ask.

"Delicious," she says, raising her eyebrows. "Yours?"

"Kind of amazing," I say, smiling. Dawn smiles back.
"Listen," I start. "I'm not going to pretend what you'd said regarding
my reasons for being here were untrue," I stare into my glass and
slowly turn it. "I'm here on business."

"And what is your business?" Dawn asks.

"It's related to locksmith work."

"You know, Jesse, the last time you and I were in town there
was a burglary not far from our motel."

"Is that so?" I say without looking up from my drink.

"Yes, that's so," she says.

I swallow hard. I feel my face and neck getting warm. I'm
hopeful the restaurant's blue lights will obscure my redness. "What
exactly are you implying?" I ask, looking her in the eyes.

She smiles and looks down at the table, shaking her head.
"I'm not going to pry, Jesse. I'll just ask this one question."

I breathe deeply and reach for my drink, wondering if this is
the moment when the date ends and she storms away from the table,
gets into her car, and leaves.

"Have you ever killed anyone?"

The moment she asks this question, I'm taking a sip of the
Purple Rose of Cairo. I nearly spit it out, but instead I cough slightly
and somehow manage to swallow. I bring my napkin to my lips,
covering my mouth.

"Are you kidding?" I ask.

Dawn shrugs.

"Look, I make a good living. I don't work a regular nine to
five job. If you're looking for someone like that, it's not me you
want. I'm not an angel, not by a longshot, but I work hard, and I like
you a lot, and no, I've never killed anyone."

Our waiter comes back to the table. "Are you ready to
order?"

I order a T-bone steak with a side of cremini mushrooms and
garlic mashed potatoes. Dawn orders the New York strip with a side
of roasted Brussels sprouts and a baked potato.

I pull out my pack of Marlboros from my suit jacket pocket.

"What are you doing?" Dawn asks.

"Hmm?" I say, as I take a cigarette out and fish around inside my pants for my Zippo.

"You can't smoke in here, Jesse."

"Oh," I say, putting the cigarette back in the pack. "Are you sure?"

Dawn laughs. "Am I sure? Yeah, I'm sure. You can't smoke in restaurants. You didn't know that?"

"I knew you couldn't smoke in certain restaurants, but I figured, you know, this is a fancier place, and I thought they'd be cool with it."

Dawn continues to laugh. "I can't tell if you're joking," she says, shaking her head.

I shrug and reach for my drink. "Were you ever a smoker?" I ask.

"No, I mean, I tried it a couple times at parties when I was younger, but it never did anything for me."

We're both quiet for a moment. I recognize Billie Holiday's song I'm Gonna Lock My Heart (and Throw Away the Key) over the restaurant's speakers.

"This is the first song I've heard since we got here that has vocals. You like jazz?" I ask.

Dawn shrugs. "Sometimes."

"My roommate plays jazz."

"Yeah?"

"He has a trio."

"You like jazz?" Dawn asks.

"I like Billie Holiday," I say.

"Is that who we're listening to?"

"Mmm hmm," I say as I take another sip of my drink.

"You're liking that drink, aren't you?" she says. I nod. "Can I try it?"

"Sure," I say, sliding the drink across the table toward her.

"Is it all right if I just…," she lifts the drink to her lips.

"Of course."

Dawns takes a tiny sip of my drink. "Whoa! That's strong," she says as she coughs and slides the drink back across the table toward me.

111

"You think?" I say, taking a sip.

"Try mine," she pushes her beverage across the table.

I pick it up and take a sip directly from the glass. Dawn's drink is fruity and sweet. I can barely taste any alcohol in it. I push it back toward her.

"Now I understand why you think mine's strong. Yours is like candy! It's super sweet."

"Come on!" she says. "It's not that sweet."

"I think I need to call my dentist."

"Your dentist?"

"Your drink just gave me a cavity," I say, holding my cheek, pretending to be in pain.

Dawn laughs. I love to watch her laugh. She doesn't hold back, opening her mouth and throwing her head back.

The meals come out, and everything smells and tastes amazing. Dawn and I continue to drink and talk more during dinner. I order a bottle of wine and pour us each a glass. We toast a second time and finish our meals, sharing our entrees with one another. After dinner, she excuses herself to use the bathroom. I figure it's a good time to step outside for a smoke.

The doorman holds the door open for me as I exit. I light a cigarette and seat myself on a nearby bench. From the street, I hear cars honking madly just before a white Toyota Yaris coupe pulls sharply into the steakhouse's parking lot. Clouds of thick, white smoke billow out of the vehicle's open driver side window. The small car rolls up onto the beautifully manicured lawn before coming to an abrupt stop.

A guy who looks to be about my age quickly exits the vehicle and pulls a phone out of his pants' pocket. The doorman walks quickly over.

"Hey!" he yells at the driver who's now fumbling with his phone. "You can't park there!"

"Can you see the smoke?" the guy asks as he holds his phone up to take a photo of the little, white car.

"Hey!" the doorman yells again as he grabs the guys phone and pushes it down. "Did you hear what I said?"

"I just need to get a photo," the driver says as he holds his phone over his head so the doorman can't grab it.

"I don't care what you need to do. Get that car out of my lot now or I'm calling the police."

The driver looks over in my direction. "Can you see it?" he yells. "Can you see the smoke?"

I look back at the car. The white smoke has all but completely vanished. "It looks okay to me," I say, taking a drag from my cigarette.

"See? Your car's fine. Now please get in it and get it out of my lot before I call the cops," the doorman says. He walks over to the car, which is still running, and opens the driver side door.

The driver sighs, pushes his phone back into his pocket, and gets into the car. The doorman slams the door shut and walks back to his post, shaking his head.

The Yaris reverses off the lawn and stops. The driver puts the car into gear and drives by me. I get a good look at the guy. He looks like he hasn't had a good night's sleep in days.

"You believe that guy?" the doorman asks as he walks by me.

I extinguish my cigarette in a nearby brass ashtray and follow the doorman back into the restaurant.

Joel brings the check, and I pay with cash.

"Cash?" Dawn asks.

"People still use cash," I say.

"Well, yeah, but I saw the prices on the menu. These dinners weren't cheap. The drinks and the wine alone must total well over fifty dollars. I'm looking around here, Jesse. This is a nice place. Do you always walk around with that much money in your wallet?"

"No, but it's the way I prefer to pay for things. What are we going to do after this?" I ask, trying to change the subject.

"Well," Dawn says. "It's a nice night, and since I'm driving, I'd like to take us someplace where we can go for a walk."

"I know a park by a lake," I say. "It's well-lit at night and there's a paved path."

"What are we waiting for?"

Dawn and I slide out of the booth. The hostess wishes us a lovely night. The man in the suit opens the door, and Dawn and I walk to her car. She pulls out of the restaurant parking lot, and we drive down the street.

"Can I smoke in your car?" I ask.

"Hell no!" she says.

I roll down the window and breathe the cool evening air in deeply as the wind hits my face. I'm slightly drunk, and when I inhale through my nose, the alcohol in my system, paired with the oxygen, creates a pleasant numbing effect. As we're driving I give Dawn directions to the lake. She rolls down her window and opens the car's sunroof.

She pulls into a parking lot. We go for a walk around the lake. It's a lovely night. Dawn and I hold hands as we stroll along the paved walkway.

"What's your favorite memory from childhood?" she asks.

"I was just thinking about this the other day."

"Only the other day?" she asks. "I pretty much live in my childhood memories. I thought everybody did."

"Some of my best memories were of my dad and me and my brother playing football at the high school after hours."

"My dad used to play football with me and my brothers in our backyard," Dawn says.

"You played football?"

"We're a big football family. Sunday afternoons during football season it was always me and my dad and my brothers on the couch, watching the Colts on TV. In the evening, we'd go out into the backyard. Dad would have us setting up plays and trying to intercept passes. It was a lot of fun."

"How many brothers do you have?"

"Two."

"Older or younger?"

"One older, one younger. I'm a *total* middle child."

"What do you mean by that?"

"I mean, I had to distinguish myself, so I went in a completely different direction than my brothers did. Working in retail…it's not the sort of thing anyone in my family had pursued."

"What kind of work did your family do?"

"A lot of them are in the food service industry. My parents ran a local sandwich shop. My brothers and I worked in the shop during the summers to make extra money. Before that, my grandfather ran a bakery. My father used to decorate cakes and deliver bagels and donuts to local businesses."

"What do your brothers do now?"

"My younger brother graduated high school, and he's working with our dad in the shop. He'll probably take it over when dad retires. My older brother runs a catering business out of his house. He's been at it for a couple years now and it's going well. He does it with his wife."

"You have any nephews and nieces?"

"My older brother and his wife have two kids, a boy and a girl. They're five and seven. I love to spoil them. How about you?'

"I've got one niece. Her name's Jolene. She's still very small. You ever think about having kids?"

"I've thought about it. Maybe one day, if I meet the right person."

We walk the circumference of the lake and end up back at Dawn's car.

"What now?" I ask.

"You could kiss me," she says.

I hold her bare shoulders and kiss her slowly and gently on the lips. Her fingers find the belt loops on my slacks and she pulls me toward her. A car pulls into the only other available space in the lot next to Dawn's. We stop kissing, and I clear my throat. We both look over at the other car. A man is in the driver's seat, running his hands through his hair. A woman in the passenger seat appears to be crying.

"Is it me, or do couples in troubled relationships seem to find us whenever we're together?" Dawn asks.

"You want to head back?" I ask.

"Yes," she says.

On our way back to the hotel, Dawn and I talk more about our families. I tell her about my brother and how both Bill and my father died in car accidents. I also talk a bit about my uncle Jake and my mother's new boyfriend. Dawn tells me about growing up in Indiana. She says she sometimes misses it.

When we get back to the motel, Dawn opens her trunk and takes her suitcase out. "Let me get that for you," I say, picking up it up. "So, we're really going to go for a swim?" I ask.

"Yeah, why not?"

"I don't know, maybe because it's after eleven o'clock and we've both been drinking?"

"Oh, come on. If I'm sober enough to drive, you're sober enough to swim. Besides, if we're not going to do it now, when would we go? Come on! It'll be fun. You brought your suit, didn't you?"

"Yeah, I brought it."

I walk Dawn's suitcase upstairs to the room. I put her luggage on one of the beds. She walks in after me and shuts the door. She looks around and puts her purse next to her suitcase and sits on the edge of the mattress. She kicks off her shoes, stands up, and begins to disrobe.

"Uh, the bathroom's right over there," I say, looking away.

"I don't mind," she says.

"Okay," I say, shrugging.

I pull the blinds shut and begin to unbutton my shirt. When I turn around, she's completely naked, going through her suitcase, looking for her bathing suit. I take off my shirt and t-shirt and unbuckle my pants as I kick my shoes off.

Dawn looks up and laughs as I walk in place to get my pants off over my feet. I smile as I watch her step into her blue and white swimsuit and pull it up over her torso and shoulders. I drop my boxer shorts and kick them up in the air with one foot, catching them with my hand mid-air. We both laugh.

"Where's your bathing suit? I'll get it for you," she says as she walks toward my duffel bag.

"No!" I say, moving in her direction with my hands out. She stops and sighs. "It's over here in my suitcase," I say. I open my suitcase and pull out a pair of red trunks. I step into my swimsuit and pull it up around my waist.

"Let me at least get the towels," she says.

116

I don't stop her as she disappears into the bathroom. She returns with the towels and tosses one to me. I catch it and wrap it around my neck. Dawn takes flip-flops out of her suitcase and drops them on the floor, slipping her feet into them.

"You ready to do this?" she asks.

"Let's go," I say as I pick up my cigarettes, lighter, and room key.

I follow her out of the room and down the stairs. As we're descending, I pull the towel from around my neck and softly hit her in the ass with it. "Hey!" she yells, turning around. I do it again and this time she grabs the towel and yanks it from my hands. She looks surprised, as if she can't believe she just took it from me. I charge at her. She screams and runs down the hall. She opens the door for the pool and pushes it closed behind her, holding it shut so I can't enter. We're both laughing hysterically. Dawn finally gives up, turns, runs across the tiled floor, and tosses my towel into the pool.

"Hey!" I yell. I've got her cornered. I take a quick look around. We're the only two people in the pool area.

"No! No! Here! You can throw my towel in!" she shouts. I yank the towel out of her hands and throw it on a chaise lounge along with my cigarettes, lighter, and the room key, then I grab her by the arms. She squats down as if waterskiing so I can't pull her forward. I climb her arms like ropes, then I grab her around the waist and put her over my shoulder. She's kicking her legs, and I can see the birthmark on the inside of her knee up close.

"What's this?" I ask, pushing it like a button. She's laughing hysterically, and I'm spinning us around. Both of her flip-flops fly off her feet. I spank her bum playfully with one hand while my other hand holds her legs.

"No! Stop it, Jesse!" she says, laughing and slapping my back with her hands as she kicks her feet.

"Hey! Cut that out! That's it. You're going in the pool." I run and jump into the pool with Dawn still over my shoulder. She screams, and we both fall under the water as if in slow motion. It's warm, and the green hue caused by the lights coming from the pool's walls is surprisingly romantic. We surface, and Dawn splashes me immediately. "Hey!" I yell. I splash her back. She swims to the other side of the pool. I ball up my soaked towel and toss it near the chaise lounge where the rest of my things are, then I swim after her. We're standing in the shallow end now, both of us out of breath. I hoist myself out of the pool and walk over to the hot tub.

I turn the knob on the wall and start the bubbles. I slide into the water and sit myself on the bench built into the side of the jacuzzi. I stare at her as she stands in the shallow end of the pool. She's looking at me, but neither of us are saying anything. She bends, takes a mouthful of water, and spits it out in my direction. I laugh a little.

"Is that your new tattoo?" she asks.

I turn my shoulder toward her. "Yep," I say. "The guy did a good job. Come over and have a look."

She steps out of the pool, walks carefully across the tiles and slowly steps down the stairs into the hot, bubbling water.

"See," I say, turning my shoulder toward her.

She wades into the tub and touches my shoulder.

"Does it hurt?" she asks.

"It's a little tender."

She puts her arms around my neck. We're both gently bouncing up and down in the water, nose to nose, squatting to keep our torsos submerged in the warmth. We turn slowly as if dancing. She wraps her legs around my waist, and I slide my hands around her lower back. I can feel her breath on my lips. We close our eyes and begin to kiss as we slowly turn. She pulls her body next to mine, and I hold her tighter, closer. Our lips slide over one another's, our mouths open. I gently bite at her lips.

The door to the pool room opens and two old women walk in wearing bathing caps. Dawn slowly untangles herself from me and floats to the other side of the tub. The women seem to take no notice of us as they put their towels on chairs and carefully get into the pool. Their voices are foreign.

Dawn slowly backs out of the hot tub, climbing the stairs backward, looking at me the entire time. I watch her move. She walks over to the chaise lounge where her towel is. I follow her out of the jacuzzi and walk over to where she's drying off. She slips on her flip-flops and hands me the wet towel. I ring it out, dry myself off as best I can, and follow her out of the pool area and up the stairs to where our room is.

I unlock the door, and we step inside. The only light in the room comes from a small table lamp in the far corner. Neither of us say a word. I shut the door and lock it. When I turn around, she's in front of me. Dawn pushes her lips against mine so hard the back of my head hits the door. She takes my hands and puts them on her chest.

My palms fit perfectly over each of her breasts, which are still covered by her swimsuit. My hands slide up to the straps on her shoulders. I pull them down. She steps closer to me, pressing her naked torso against my own. I kiss her neck as my hands continue to push her wet swimsuit over her hips and off her body. She kicks it away.

As we continue to kiss, my hands explore her nakedness. Her breathing gets heavier as I place tiny kisses on her neck and shoulder. I feel her thumbs slide into my waistband just before she pushes my swim trunks down around my thighs. They fall to the carpet, and I kick them away.

Both of us are completely naked. The kisses grow more passionate, our tongues playing in each other's mouths. We move toward the bed. I push her suitcase and purse off the mattress and lay her down on top of the covers. I lie on my side next to her with one arm under her neck as she lies on her back. I touch her with my right hand, slowly moving my fingers in circles on her most intimate area. Her body responds to my touch. She tilts her head back and moans. Her legs slowly part.

We kiss as she plays with her breasts, pulling on her small, erect nipples as I continue to fondle her. She opens her eyes and pushes me onto my back. She straddles me, rubbing herself over my hard member. She leans forward, taking my hands in hers, kissing my neck, her wet hair falling over my face. She sits up and again places my hands over her breasts.

With one hand, she reaches between our bodies and places me at her entrance. She then eases back. I feel myself being completely enveloped by her softness. She begins to move her hips, her hands on my chest. I grip her thighs, moving in rhythm as she rides me. She grinds faster and harder, pushing her hips back and forth so that I'm sliding in and out with little effort on my part. She inhales sharply and presses her lips to mine. I feel her entire body shake just before she exhales and falls on me.

I roll toward her. We both stand. I turn her around and put both of her hands against the wall above her head. With one hand, I reach between her thighs. I kiss her neck and behind her ear. With my other hand, I touch her breasts.

She throws her head back. I slide myself completely inside. She gasps. I begin to push hard, panting into her ear. She moves her feet closer to the wall to stay balanced, moaning louder now and pushing back, meeting my every thrust. I finish and fall onto the bed.

She walks out of view. On the ceiling, I see the light from the bathroom. I hear her peeing. I stand, stretch, and slowly walk over.

I wash my hands and face in the sink and clean myself with a tissue. Dawn flushes the toilet.

"Whoa," she says, looking at me.

We both smile.

We lay naked, side by side, in silence for a long time, her head on my chest. After she rolls onto her back, I get up, pull my boxers on, and go out on the deck for a smoke. I have a slight hangover from the alcohol. The door slides open and Dawn steps out. She's completely dressed, wearing jeans, a red t-shirt, and white sneakers.

"Thank you for a great night," she says, hugging me and giving me a small kiss on the cheek.

"Are you okay to drive?" I ask.

"Yeah, I'm okay," she says.

"Are you sure you don't want to spend the night?"

"I'd love to, but I've got to be back to open the store."

"You need help with your suitcase?"

"I think I can handle it," she says.

I watch her collect her things. She turns and blows me a kiss before walking out of the room. I pretend to catch it. Moments later, over the railing of the deck, I watch as she gets in her car, starts it, and pulls out of the parking lot and onto the street. I feel lonelier than I ever have in my entire life.

THE HEAVINESS

The sun's rays shining through the blinds in front of the sliding glass door make me miserable. I don't want to face the day. I feel so alone. I wish the sun would disappear and leave me in darkness, at least that's where I was the last time I was happy. It's as if the memory of my entire evening with Dawn is being burned away by that giant sphere of fire we're all hopelessly, ceaselessly rolling around.

I try pulling the covers over my head and curling myself into a ball, but I can still hear the dreaded sounds of a new day. Doors open and close. Car engines start before fading away as they exit the parking lot. Dress shoes make their way down the hall to a continental breakfast being offered in the lobby.

I'm in absolute misery. I can't decide if it's because I'm ashamed of who I am or if it's because…no, that's it. I'm ashamed of who I am. I think back to my conversation with my uncle Jake. Was I being honest about sleeping with a clear conscience? How many more jobs before something goes wrong? Will I know when to walk away from the table? Was it ever about the money for me? I don't think it was. This, I think to myself, is the heaviness.

The sun is like a spotlight, highlighting the wicked and the guilty and the criminals and the sinners and the worst of humanity. There's nothing wonderful about it. All those songs and poems and sayings and clichés about the sun and its power are bullshit.

I envy the white insects that live under rocks and tree stumps, and the ghostly, transparent fish that swim just above the cold ocean floor where the sun never shines.

The sun is a reminder that life is passing. The sun is a reminder that your days are numbered. The sun says, "Here I am, you bastards. I'm going to blaze my fiery might on all of you whether you want it or not. You can't hide from me forever. I won't let you live in darkness.

I remember going to dances in junior high. I'd walk out to my mother's car in the dark. The gymnasium would be romantically lit, but still dark. I had no qualms about letting go in the dark. There, with friends, we would dare each other to ask girls in our class to dance. We would sing along to the songs that defined us, the music

121

that was meant to be listened to at night. Our generation's anthems were conceived and recorded at night in dark studios in the small hours of the morning while it was still black as pitch outside. Then, as if to make fools of us all, the music would stop at the end of the evening and the lights would come on.

The sun is like those lights in the gymnasium in junior high after a dance. It's cruel and makes you remember the ugliness of everything. It reminds you there isn't any magic, not really. At least not in the day.

The rain is a friend. The rain and the clouds, obscuring the world and making everything appear as if it's the same shade. God, what I would give for a rainy day right now.

I throw the covers off and attempt to shut the blinds tighter to block out any light coming through. It's useless. The sun still finds a way in.

I take my cigarettes into the bathroom. I don't turn on the light. I shut the door, and, using my lighter, find my way to the tub, climbing in. A tiny puddle of water on the porcelain soaks through my boxers. It's cold on the underside of my thigh. I light a cigarette. I'm not supposed to be smoking in the motel room, but there's no way I'm going to face the sun. Not today.

I fall asleep. Ashes from my cigarette float down a thin river of bathwater, circling the drain. The filter of the extinguished butt sits on the edge of the tub. After a while, I get up and put on jeans, a gray sweatshirt, a black baseball hat with the Public Enemy logo on it, and sunglasses, and I walk through the hall and downstairs.

In the motel lobby, I ask the clerk for the menu of the nearest sandwich shop. She gives me a brochure for a place called Sub Mission. I thank her and ask to use the phone. She seems surprised that I don't have one in my pocket. I call the sandwich shop and place an order for a large BLT grinder, an order of fries with plenty of ketchup, and a grape soda.

The kid on the other end of the phone tells me it's going to be fifteen minutes. I hang up and take a seat in one of the cushioned lobby chairs. I'm still wearing the cap and sunglasses. I want a cigarette, but I don't want to walk outside. You couldn't pay me to walk outside while that yellow son of a bitch is in the sky.

I watch men with briefcases come into the motel, assumedly traveling on business. I see families with kids and old couples on vacation. They look at me and immediately look away. After less than fifteen minutes, a kid from Sub Mission shows up with my order. I call him over to where I'm seated. He gives me the bag. I pay him three times the cost of the meal.

I take the food upstairs and climb back into the tub. I stand my lit Zippo on the edge of the bathtub for light as I unwrap my sandwich and eat it along with the fries. I make a puddle of ketchup on a napkin between my legs and dip the fries in it. When I'm done, I throw all the paper and napkins onto the bathroom floor.

I stare into the darkness and sing, "I'm gonna lock my heart, and throw away the key, I'm wise to all, those tricks you played on me, I'm gonna turn my back on love, gonna snog the moon above, seal all my windows up with tin, so the love bug can't get in."

THROUGH THE ROOF

I dream I'm on an exercise bike on the second floor of a gym in the city. I'm wearing black bicycle shorts and a tight, yellow t-shirt, clothes I have never owned in my waking life. The row of stationary bikes faces a window that looks out over a busy street. A lit cigarette sits in an ashtray affixed between the handlebars of the bike.

As I peddle, I balance a plate of small chocolate donuts on my lap. I eat them one at a time. After finishing each one, I take a drag from the cigarette before placing it back in the ashtray. I never stop pedaling.

I'm woken by the phone. I get out of the tub, walk into the room, and answer it.

"Hello?" I say.

"Kid."

"Frank?"

"Yeah," he says. "You eat dinner yet?"

"Not yet."

"Come to the abandoned building across from the motel in an hour. I'll have a pizza."

"Okay, I'll be there," I say.

I brush the crumbs from lunch off my shirt and set the alarm on my watch to go off in an hour. I clean myself up in the sink before putting my toiletries and clothing back into my suitcase.

After an hour, my watch alarm goes off. I pick up my duffel bag and suitcase and leave the room. My back is stiff from having slept on the hard, cold porcelain for so long.

I walk out of the motel and across the parking lot. The sun is going down. I take off my shades, put them in my bag, and stroll across the street to the abandoned warehouse.

As I enter, I see a single glowing lightbulb hanging from a wire over a table. Frank and Walt are sitting across from one another, eating pizza and drinking beer out of bottles.

"Jeez, you look like shit," Walt says as he takes a bite out of a slice.

"How you been, kid?" Frank asks.

"I've been better," I say.

"Woman trouble?" Frank asks.

"How could you tell?"

"By the time you're my age, you can tell," he says.

I drop my stuff near the door and walk over to where Frank and Walt are sitting. I open a metal folding chair and sit myself at the table. I pull a slice of pepperoni pizza out of the box and take a bite. It's barely warm.

"What have you been up to the last twenty-four hours?" Walt asks.

"Sleeping in a bathtub," I say.

"That's a metaphor if I ever heard one," Frank says.

"I wish it was," I say as I reach across the table, grab a bottle of beer, and twist off the cap.

"What's the plan, Frank?" Walt asks.

Frank looks at Walt as if he's just been insulted. "Why don't you just relax and enjoy the pizza," Frank says. Walt shrugs and takes a swig of beer. "Spill it, kid," Frank says. "Tell us what's going on in the pussy department."

I sigh and run my hand through my hair. "I met this woman, and we seemed to really hit it off. We had a great night together, and the sex was amazing, and..."

"Wait," Walt says with a mouthful of pizza. "No *and*, you just skipped over the best part. What made the sex amazing?"

"Don't tell him, kid," Frank says. "I never kissed and told, and it always served me better."

"Didn't you just ask Jesse what's going on in the pussy department?" Walt asks. When he gets no response, he whispers, "Whatever," and takes another slug of beer.

I've eaten two slices of pizza and drank two beers before Frank's ready to talk about how things are going to go tonight.

"All right, boys, let's clear off this table and get down to business," he says.

Walt and I clear the pizza and bottles, and Frank pulls a map out of a cardboard tube and rolls it out on the table in front of us.

"This is the lay of the land," he says as Walt and I lean in. "This is where we're going in."

"The roof?" I ask.

"That's right," Frank says.

"Pardon me, Frank," Walt says. "But where are we getting the equipment to break into a jewelry store through the roof?"

"You'll see when we get there," Frank says.

"Why wouldn't the guy who's tipping you off just leave the backdoor unlocked?" Walt asks.

"Maybe because the whole place is wired with an alarm system that will go off if any doors or windows are broken or opened, smart guy!" Frank shouts.

"Does this mean we'll have to exit through the roof?" I ask.

"It does," Frank says.

Walt and I both sigh. I picture my heavy duffel bag being hoisted up through the roof of a building. I don't know how I'm supposed to carry it up by myself. I can't imagine how we're going to get the loot out through the roof, but I trust Frank. He has yet to get us pinched or have a job cut short due to a mistake in judgement or misinformation.

After Frank shows us on the map where we'll be entering and how we'll locate the safe, he tells us to get our equipment ready. While Walt goes through his detonation material, I go through my bag and make sure I've got everything I need to do my part of the job.

"How much did Frank tell you we were walking away with?"

"Is this a test?"

Walt laughs. "I just want to make sure we're getting the same thing is all."

"He told me the job will pay ten grand," I say.

"Hmmm," Walt says as he rubs the side of his face

I can tell that Walt's been told the same thing, but he was hoping I'd give him a different answer so he'd have something to bitch about.

"You gonna ask how much he's taking?" Walt asks.

"None of my business," I say.

"Ain't you the least bit curious?"

I shrug. Walt zips up his backpack and carries it over to the door. I zip up my duffel bag, pick up my suitcase, and follow him. Frank is outside. The van's running.

Walt turns back and looks at me before opening the door. "You got everything?"

I look down at my gear. "Yep," I say.

"Let's do this," Walt says. He kicks the door open. It swings wide. I follow him through it quickly to avoid my bag and suitcase getting stuck. The door slams shut behind me.

As I march to the van, I take a last look at the motel across the street. The lights are on in the indoor pool area, but I can't make out any people swimming or enjoying the hot tub. I think about Dawn and the good time we had the other night. Walt pulls open the van's side door and throws his backpack in.

"I'm driving," he says as he steps in and sits down behind the wheel. I push my duffel bag and suitcase into the van and climb in. I slide the side door shut and make myself as comfortable as I can.

Walt puts the van in gear and heads down the road. Frank gives directions while looking at an unfolded map. Walt lights a cigarette. I can't remember if Frank told him not to smoke. It's probably safer if I don't light up since I'm sitting next to Walt's backpack.

We drive for about forty minutes before we pull into a dark strip mall. Frank tells Walt to pull around back.

Walt parks our vehicle and kills the engine. He and Frank exit the van on either side. I slide the side door open. Frank turns on a high-powered flashlight. Walt and I follow him to the building with our gear. He stops when he gets to a long metal ladder lying along a wall.

"All right, you two," Frank barks. "Get that ladder up against the wall."

I put my duffel bag down, and Walt and I pick up the ladder and lean it against the brick exterior. It's not tall enough to reach the roof. I push the feet of the ladder closer to the wall so that it's practically standing straight up. Walt pulls a rope attached to the ladder so that the top portion slides upward. It's loud, but none of the neighboring businesses in the plaza are open, and even if there are cameras watching us, it's too dark for them to get a decent view of our faces. As Walt continues to pull the rope, extending the ladder, a metal hook in the center grabs onto each rung as it passes. Frank focuses the beam of his powerful flashlight upward so we can see when the top of the ladder reaches the roof. As soon as it does, Walt stops pulling the rope. The ladder is now resting against the top corner of the building.

"All right, me first," Frank says. "Hold the ladder, kid." He puts the powerful flashlight through a loop on his wide leather utility belt and begins to climb. I hold the ladder steady with both hands as Frank climbs, rung after rung, until he disappears over the edge of the roof. "You next, Walt," Frank yells down.

Walt climbs up the ladder while I hold it steady. As soon as he disappears over the edge of the roof, it's my turn. I pick up my heavy duffel bag and pull the strap over my head and across the front of my body so that the bag is slung diagonally across my back. It's heavy and makes climbing the ladder awkward. I don't know why I'm the last to go up, but I don't complain. I climb the ladder as Walt holds it steady from the roof. When I get to the top, both Walt and Frank grab my arms and pull me over the edge.

"All right," Frank says. "Follow me."

We follow him to a sky window. From a leather sheath in his belt, he pulls out a rubber handle and extends a telescopic piece of metal from its center that resembles a thick antenna. He motions for me to come over to where he's squatting. Frank pries the tool under the edge of the glass and pops it out of the wooden frame.

"Get your fingers under there, kid," Frank says.

I put my duffel bag down and slide my fingers underneath the glass. It's heavy and the edge isn't rounded. Frank walks around to the other side and pries it up. He motions for Walt to come over. Walt squats down and slides his fingers under the opposite edge of the glass.

"Okay," Frank says. "On three, you guys lift it up and put it over on my right."

Frank counts to three, and Walt and I slowly stand with the glass in our hands. Even with gloves on, the edge hurts my fingers. We walk to the right side of Frank and put the glass down gently.

"Okay, good," he says. "Now we need the ladder that we climbed up here on.

Walt sighs exasperatedly. "Are you kidding?"

Frank just looks at Walt as he points the flashlight beam at the top of the ladder which is peeking over the lip of the roof. I walk over to the edge and wait for Walt by the ladder. He looks pissed that he has to do so much manual labor before we even get inside to rob the place.

Walt and I pull the ladder up in stages. We each grip a side and nod at one another, and then we hoist it as high as we can before pulling up the next section. As soon as it's more than halfway in the air, the top half see-saws down and lands on the roof with a clang. Walt and I each take a side of the ladder and walk it all the way onto the roof so the end of it is waiting at the lip of the window.

"Okay, now put that son of a bitch through the frame and be sure to ease it down *slowly*," Frank says. He watches us as he points his flashlight at the glassless opening.

Walt and I retract the ladder as much as possible before lowering it through the space where the sky window was. I hold the metal hook back while he walks the ladder toward me, slowly bringing it back to the size it was when we first found it. Frank huffs impatiently.

"This is the only way to do it, Frank," Walt says.

"Just hurry up!" the old man says angrily.

When the ladder is finally back to its original size, we each grab a side and begin to lower it through the opening. Frank shines his flashlight down into the room. We let the ladder out until the bottom half finds the floor, then we throw the hook, locking it and making sure it's secure.

"I'll go down first," Frank says.

"Fine with me," Walt mutters, loud enough for only me to hear.

With the flashlight in his belt, Frank slowly descends the ladder into the jewelry store through the opening in the roof. When he gets to the bottom, he tells me to lower my duffel bag. I lower it down to him, dangling it by the shoulder strap until it's resting in his waiting hands.

"All right, you come down first, kid," Frank commands.

The first thing I notice as I'm stepping down the ladder into the jewelry store is the coldness. "They must have had the air conditioning on today or something," I say.

Frank ignores me as he holds the ladder for Walt. As soon as Walt's inside, Frank turns his flashlight's beam toward me and says, "Let's go."

Walt and I follow Frank through what looks like a back-office area.

"Is this place alarmed at all?" Walt asks.

"Only the main floor area," Frank says. "If we tried to exit through the store itself, the motion sensors would detect us before we got halfway to the front. There aren't any motion sensors in this office area. The inside man assured me the cameras outside the building would be deactivated during the job. The safe is right over here."

Walt and I follow Frank's beam. I'm carrying my duffel bag. Built into a wall behind a desk is a small door with a brass handle in the middle. Frank pulls it open to reveal a new-looking combination safe. I don't recognize the brand. There are certain universalities regarding safes, however, and I'm certain that I'll be able to find the important places on this one to drill into in order that Walt's able to do his thing.

Frank moves out of the way as I kneel and assemble my equipment. I hand Walt the extension cord, and he walks it over to an outlet to get me some power. I put the drill down beside me and take out my stethoscope and headlamp. Then, with a small pickax, I begin tapping different places on the face of the safe, managing to find three spots that should be suitable for Walt to plant his explosives that will do the least amount of damage to whatever's inside.

I mark my spots on the face of the safe with a piece of orange chalk. When I'm done, I start drilling. Frank and Walt are sitting in swivel chairs, arguing about sports, when I push my first hole completely through. They stop talking and come over to examine my work.

"Keep going, kid," Frank says.

I continue to drill until I've made three holes in the safe. By the time I'm done, Frank and Walt have stopped talking about sports and are describing all the car accidents they've been in.

"Okay, my part's done. You're up," I say to Walt as I put my tools back into the duffel bag and move out of the way.

I plant myself in the chair Walt had been sitting in. I light a cigarette and watch him do his thing.

Walt packs the holes I've made with plastic explosives and wires them to blow from a detonator. His part of the job takes maybe twenty minutes. Frank looks at his watch and yawns.

"What time is it?" I ask.

"It's about that time," Frank says, winking.

"You guys ready to rock and roll?" Walt asks.

Frank and I walk to the back of the room and squat behind a desk. Walt strings the wire from the explosives over the carpet and the desk and squats down next to us. He hits the button on the detonator. There's a quick sizzling sound followed by a loud bang as the door to the safe flies off and slams into a desk directly in front of it. A printer falls off the desk and smashes on the floor.

There's some smoke, but not enough to cause concern. Walt holds the flashlight while Frank takes one of the canvas sacks from his belt and begins filling it with the contents of the safe. As soon as the first sack's full, he hands it to me. Frank takes the other sack off his belt and continues to unload the safe. After the safe is emptied completely, he hands the second sack to me.

"Why does Jesse get to hold the sacks?" Walt complains.

"Because you've got enough to worry about," Frank says. "Tie those up real tight," Frank says, taking one of the sacks from me and using the open end to tie it closed on itself like a balloon before dropping it at my feet.

I follow his lead, firmly knotting the other sack's opening.

"Follow me," he says. I follow Frank to the ladder. "When I get up there, throw each sack up to me."

I watch Frank slowly climb the ladder, taking the flashlight up with him on his belt, leaving Walt and I in the store. After Frank disappears onto the roof, Walt and I are standing side by side in complete darkness at the bottom of the ladder.

"How much you think we got?" he asks.

"I don't know," I say. "I guess it depends on the size of the bills, right?"

"Throw those sacks up to me, kid," Frank says from the roof. After I toss the sacks up, Walt climbs the ladder.

"I need to grab my equipment, Frank. I can't see anything down here," I say.

Frank huffs, annoyed. "Okay, I'm dropping the flashlight. Get ready for it."

I wait at the bottom of the ladder. Frank drops the flashlight and it lands in my hands like a football. I walk back into the area where we were working and find my duffel bag. I zip it closed and throw the strap across my torso. I walk back to the ladder. Frank is waiting at the top with his hands on his knees, looking down at me.

"I'm going to toss up the flashlight," I say.

I underhand it to Frank. He catches it then holds the ladder as I climb. When I get to the top, I see Walt looking nervously over the edge of the building, his backpack on his back. Walt walks to the other end of the building and looks out.

"What the hell are you doing?" Frank asks.

"Huh? Nothing," Walt says. He comes over to where Frank and I are standing and grabs the ladder. "Let's haul this thing up," he says to me.

I drop my duffel bag and help Walt lift the ladder. We carry it directly over to the edge of the building and lower it down to the parking lot below. Walt immediately begins to descend.

"When I get to the bottom, throw me the sacks," he says to Frank.

We watch Walt descend. I look at Frank, skeptical that he'll do what Walt has asked.

When Walt reaches the bottom of the ladder, Frank tosses the two sacks of cash over the edge of the building. Walt catches first one and then the other. He sets the sacks down next to each other in the parking lot and immediately pulls the ladder away from the edge of the building. Frank lunges, attempting to grab it, but he's unable to reach it in time.

"You son of a bitch!" Frank shouts.

The ladder falls in the parking lot with a loud, reverberating clang. We watch Walt pick up the sacks of cash and run to the van. He gets into the driver side, starts the engine, and drives away with the score and my suitcase.

"Goddamn it!" Frank yells.

"Now what?" I ask.

"We gotta get the hell outta here. If that piece of shit has two brain cells, he'll stop at the first payphone and call the cops on us."

"Okay," I say. "But I assume exiting through the front means we set off the alarms."

"Yeah," Frank says, rubbing his chest and looking down.

"Do we have a choice?"

"No," he says, shaking his head.

"Okay, then I'll drop down into the store first and find something to put under the opening." I lie flat on my stomach and slowly back myself through the space where the glass used to be. When I get to the edge, I dangle, holding onto the roof with my fingers before letting go. I land on my feet and immediately fall onto my ass, rolling backward. "Drop the flashlight," I say.

"No," Frank says.

"Frank, we don't have much time. We have to work together." I can tell he's lost faith in his crew and is now paranoid. "Please," I say. "Trust me."

He drops the flashlight down to me followed by my duffel bag, which he lowers slowly by the strap. I use the flashlight to find a desk and push it under the opening in the ceiling.

"All right. Come on down," I say.

Frank is slow, but he eventually gets onto his belly and slides backward through the opening in the roof. His legs are dangling in front of me. I grab him around the knees and help get him lowered onto the desk. As soon as we're both inside, I jump off the desk and throw my bag over my shoulder.

"Do you remember the route through the store?" I ask as I help Frank off the desk.

"Yeah, I remember," he says. "But we may have an issue when we get to the front door. Bring one of these chairs."

I pick up one of the heavy desk chairs.

"You ready?" I ask.

"Let's go!" he yells.

I follow Frank and his flashlight as he walks quickly out of the back-office area. As soon as we step into the store, we hear a high-pitched noise followed by the glow of a red light above us.

"This way!" Frank yells, moving through the aisles. I follow, carrying the chair in front of myself. It's heavy, and I consider putting it down and rolling it, but I'm afraid It'll get stuck on one of the corners of the jewelry cabinets.

Sirens begin to go off. Every light in the store turns on. It's the end of the junior high dance all over again. We get to the front doors, and Frank tries to push them open from the inside without success.

"You're up, kid!" he says, moving out of the way.

I drop my duffel bag from over my shoulder and pick the heavy chair up. I begin swinging it roughly at the glass with all my might, the chair's wheels and metal base crack the glass each time it makes contact. After about three swings, the door's window shatters, falling away in an S-shaped sheet. I drop the chair, pick up my bag, and carefully step through the window frame before helping Frank do the same.

We run across the parking lot and into the woods. In the distance, I hear police sirens.

"What's the plan?" I ask.

"The plan is we keep walking," Frank says.

We move through the woods for what feels like an hour and a half before we emerge in a suburban backyard. Frank is still holding the flashlight. I follow him to the driveway. He tries the doors to two cars, but neither one is unlocked. We walk into a neighboring driveway and again have no luck finding an unlocked vehicle. Next, Frank tries the side door of a garage and it opens. We walk in to find an old Buick. Frank opens the driver side door.

I open the back door, and throw my duffel bag in. I sit down in the passenger seat and watch as Frank rummages through the glove compartment and then the center console. "Bingo!" he says as he proudly holds up a single key, coincidentally attached to a lucky rabbit's foot keychain. He starts the engine and hits a button on a plastic box attached to the sun visor. The garage door slowly opens. While he's adjusting the car's rearview mirror, he suddenly stops.

"Hand me that bag in the backseat."

"My bag?" I ask.

"No, the paper bag that's back there."

I reach back and grab a paper bag that has the top rolled closed. I hand it to Frank. He unrolls the top of the bag, looks inside, and then set it at his feet.

As soon as there's enough room for the car to exit through the garage, Frank puts the Buick in gear and steps on it. We pull out onto the street. I look back at the house, but it doesn't appear anyone inside is aware of what's just happened. Frank steps on the accelerator as he turns corners, trying his best to quickly navigate us out of the suburban neighborhood and onto the highway.

"Where are we headed?" I ask.

"The city."

"How the hell am I supposed to get home?"

"You'll have to take a taxi, kid," Frank says. "We need to disappear, and the best place to do that is in the city."

I sigh and sit back. There are very few cars on the road, but Frank is careful to go the speed limit on the highway. After a while, I get the courage to ask Frank a question regarding the botched heist.

"Is this the first time something like this has happened on a job you've been on?"

"No," he says, sighing. "When I was a younger man, I was on a job with a crew of four, including myself and the boss. One of the guys tried to take off with more than he was supposed to get. I was the one who saw him beat feet through the back door of the joint. I alerted the boss. The three of us ran out after him." Frank's quiet.

"What happened?" I ask.

"We chased him into a shallow stream in some nearby woods. The boss pulled a handgun out and shot the poor bastard in the back of the head while he was trying to get away."

"Jesus," I say.

"I didn't know our boss had a piece on him."

"If you'd known he was carrying, would you have fingered the guy trying to get away?"

Frank's quiet for a moment. He sighs and runs his hand down his face. "I ask myself that question every day."

As we drive, the highway lamps cast fleeting reflections and shadows inside the old car. I light a cigarette. Frank doesn't complain. I roll down the window and watch the world go by. I think of Dawn and wonder if I'll ever see her again. I imagine there were cameras inside the jewelry store and once those lights went on, our faces were probably caught on tape and are sure to be broadcast everywhere. This is my last thought as I doze off.

I'm woken by Frank shouting, "Well I'll be a son of a bitch!"

I rub my eyes and sit up in the passenger seat. We're still on the highway. The white van is on the side of the road just ahead of us, apparently with a flat tire as it appears to be leaning to one side. Frank pulls over just ahead of it and we both get out. He leaves the engine of the Buick running. Before I can get my seatbelt off, Frank is inside the van. I run to the open side door.

"He's gone! The money's gone!" Frank shouts angrily.

My suitcase is still in the back. I step up into the van and pick it up. Frank crawls between the front seats, looks around, and exits through the driver side door, shutting it as he curses.

"Kid! Get the hell out of there!" I hear Frank shout.

I look to my right, through the windshield, and see the hood of the van is opened slightly, smoke drifting upward. I look around the van, remembering Walt's yellow backpack. "Oh shit!" I say as I jump out with my suitcase.

As I'm running past the front of the vehicle, I turn to see wires hanging over the grill. They appear to have been pulled under the van lengthwise and rigged to plastic explosives where the gas tank resides.

I catch up to Frank and jump into the passenger seat with my suitcase on my lap. Just as we both get inside and shut the doors, the van explodes in a horrible, hot, flaming ball of fire. The light from the flames illuminates the highway and the inside of the Buick as if it's the middle of a sunny day. Even though I'm sitting inside a car with the doors closed, I'm able to feel the heat from the exploding van on the side of my face.

Frank guns the Buick's engine and peels out onto the highway. He's no longer obeying the speed limit.

After twenty minutes, we see a figure on the side of the road, walking with his thumb out, hitchhiking. The figure is wearing a yellow backpack, and he's carrying two sacks over one shoulder. My heart is racing. Frank cuts the wheel and aims our car directly for Walt. The Buick hits the guardrail. Sparks fly everywhere as we grind along the steel barrier. I'm holding on for dear life as the most earsplitting sound of metal on metal fills my ears.

Walt jumps over the guardrail and disappears down an embankment. Frank slams the brakes. My side of the car is pinned against the guardrail and I can't get out. I slide across the seat and exit through the driver side. I step on an empty paper bag and run around the car to see that Frank has climbed over the guardrail and is now scurrying down the embankment in pursuit of Walt. I follow.

In the glow of a highway lamp, I watch as Walt, close to reaching the bottom of the embankment, trips on a tree root and falls, somersaulting down the hill. He only stops rolling when his head smashes against a tree, seemingly knocking him unconscious.

Frank and I get down to where Walt is laying. Frank picks up the two sacks of cash and tells me to get back up the embankment. I turn and begin climbing the steep incline, using my hands and feet.

I'm near the top when I turn and see Frank struggling to walk up the hill, the two sacks of cash held in front of him. Just beyond Frank I see Walt, now awake, slowly and groggily making his way up the hill on his hands and knees. There's blood running down one side of Walt's face, his teeth are clenched, and he's climbing with all his might.

The old man is slow. The two sacks filled with dough aren't making Frank's ascension any easier as he struggles to get back to the top of the embankment using only his feet. He's leaning forward, doing his best to remain upright, but every now and again he slides backward and must put one hand in the grass to remain in a standing position. Walt uses these opportunities to shorten the distance between himself and the cash.

Frank finally loses his footing completely and falls onto his side. As he slides backward, his ankle find's Walt's outstretched hand. Frank attempts to kick himself free without success. Walt holds Frank's leg down firmly and reaches up with his other hand, grabbing one of the sacks, yanking it from Frank's grasp, and throwing it down the embankment behind him. As Frank continues to kick, Walt grabs the second sack from Frank's hand and tosses it down the embankment and into the darkness below.

His hands now free, Frank reaches back and pulls a revolver out of his waistband. As soon as Walt sees the gun, he turns, scrambles to his feet, and begins running down the hill, stopping only to pick up both sacks of cash.

I hear a loud pop and see a flash of light and a puff of smoke. A bullet finds the back of Walt's knee. He buckles and falls face-first into the dirt. Frank stands, exhausted. He lifts the back of his shirt, tucks the revolver back into the waistband of his pants, and makes his way down to where the wounded man is lying. Walt is trying to stand on his one good leg when Frank comes up behind him and steps on the back of his knee where the bullet entered. Walt screams out in pain and falls onto his stomach. With his other foot, Frank steps on Walt's hand, causing him to let go of the money. Frank picks the two sacks up and kicks Walt in the face. He turns and walks back up the embankment with the cash.

I watch from the other side of the guardrail as Walt again struggles to get up on his one good leg, dragging his other behind him. He slowly disappears into the darkness of the woods. Frank makes his way back up to the street, and I help him over the metal barricade.

"Get your stuff. We're thumbing it from here," he says.

Frank carries the two sacks of money over one shoulder as he makes his way down the highway. I follow, walking backward with my duffel bag strung across my back. My left hand holds my suitcase while my right hand extends across the breakdown lane, my thumb in the air, attempting to flag a ride down for us. It doesn't take long before a guy in an SUV pulls over. Frank climbs into the passenger seat and I get in the back.

"Where you guys headed?" the driver asks.

"The city," Frank says. "You?"

"Same," the man says. "What's in the sacks?"

"You get us into the city safely and I'll show you," Frank says. The guy looks at Frank quizzically.

"Trust me, it'll be worth it," I say from the backseat.

The driver looks at me in his rearview mirror. I give him a sincere nod. He looks back at the road and continues to drive us into the city. The driver attempts to make small talk with Frank, but the old man isn't having it. He basically grunts while the guy tells him boring stories about his travels. Whenever the guy asks Frank a question, I do my best to give him a vague answer so Frank doesn't have to speak.

After about a half hour, we reach the city. The driver pulls off the highway, and we find ourselves in bumper to bumper traffic, hitting every light. We're passing a park when Frank says, "This'll do."

"Are you sure?" the guy asks. Frank just grunts.

The driver pulls the SUV over. I open the rear door and step out with my duffel bag and suitcase. I watch Frank untie one of the sacks, reach in, and pull out a thick stack of fifty dollar bills, handing it to the driver. The look on the man's face is priceless.

As Frank gets out of the car, the revolver falls out of the back of his pants and makes a loud clattering as it hits the street. Frank casually picks up the gun, lifts his shirt, and tucks it into the waistband of his pants. "You never picked us up, understand?" he says to the driver.

The guy nods. "You fellas have a nice night," he says.

Frank throws the sacks of cash over his shoulder and closes the passenger door. The SUV pulls back out into the city traffic.

"Come on. I'll buy you a coffee," Frank says.

We walk into an all-night diner, and Frank orders us two coffees at the counter. There are plenty of available stools, but neither one of us sits. In the unflattering lights of the diner, I see Frank's shirt and pants are covered in dirt from falling on the embankment.

"Frank."

"What?" he says, turning around.

"Maybe we should put those sacks in my duffel bag," I suggest. "There's plenty of room." A pair of suspicious-looking young guys walk by us, staring at the sacks Frank's holding. "You know, just to be safe," I add. I can tell Frank's paranoid about me walking around with the entire haul from the job. "Look," I say. "You can carry my bag if you don't trust me." I put my duffel down next to Frank's feet and step back.

"Two hot coffees!" the girl behind the counter calls out, putting two steaming white mugs in front of us.

Frank pays for the coffees, then turns, unzips my duffel bag, and puts the two sacks of cash inside. "You carry it," he says.

I pick up my bag and throw the strap over my shoulder. Frank takes his change and hands me one of the mugs. We share a spoon, stirring cream and sugar into the hot java.

Neither of us speaks as we finish our coffees without sitting down. "Follow me into the bathroom," he says.

Inside the single occupant men's room, I put my duffel bag and suitcase on the floor between us. Frank locks the bathroom door and unzips my bag. He takes out the two sacks of cash and unties one. He reaches in, pulls out thick stacks of fifties, and hands them to me.

"This is twice as much as you gave me last time," I say as I count it.

"That's yours *and* Walt's share. That son of a bitch is lucky he got away with his life. If I ever see him on the street, he better cross to the other side."

We're both quiet for a moment as I put the money into my bag, zip it closed, and throw the strap over my shoulder.

"Where will you go?" I ask.

"My sister lives in the city," he says. I look up at him, remembering the overheard phone conversation. "I'm going to get a nice hotel room and call her in the morning. See if I can visit her."

"What about the job?"

"What about it?"

"Well, all the lights went on before we could get out of the store. Maybe they have our faces on video."

"Maybe," Frank says casually.

"Well, if they have our faces, they could be after us," I say.

"Could be," he says.

"Well, should I get a haircut? Should I leave the country?" I ask.

"Do what you like."

"What are you gonna do?" I ask.

Frank puts the sacks of cash on the bathroom floor, reaches behind himself, and pulls the pistol out of the waistband of his slacks. I gasp and step backward. I swallow hard, terrified he's going to shoot me and leave my corpse in the bathroom of this diner. Instead, he sets the revolver down on the closed toilet seat lid, opens the cover on the tank, drops the gun into the water, and replaces the top.

Frank picks up the two sacks of cash, turns to me, and says, "I'm going to call the inside man and tell him he doesn't get paid until he destroys any evidence of us being there."

HOME

I take a taxi from the diner back to the duplex. I think about Walt and wonder if he managed to limp into an emergency room. I know I'll never hear from him again, and I'm okay with that.

The driver pulls onto my street. I pay the woman for the ride and give her a decent tip. I take my duffel bag and suitcase out of the cab's trunk and walk up the front stairs of the house. The sun will be up soon.

I walk upstairs and unlock the front door. The house is quiet. I toss my keys onto the table, step into my bedroom, and shut the door. I drop my stuff at the foot of my bed and turn on the stereo.

Through the speakers comes an odd collage of quirky samples and loops. The only kids they'll let DJ at this odd hour are the freaks and weirdos who enjoy creating odd pastiches of audio for their own pleasure, entrapping insomniacs who are just coherent enough to switch on a radio. I lie on my bed and turn the volume down so the noise is just barely perceptible.

I fall asleep and dream I'm a passenger in a small propeller-driven plane, flying high above a desert. As I look out the window, I see buffalo and horse and bison and sheep and goats, all running. The sun is setting. I look ahead to see what the animals are running toward, and my eyes find a stunning oasis, the setting sun's rays reflecting off it like diamonds. As we fly over, I see a mirror image of the plane in the water. Just as we're about to fly too far forward and out of view, the first of the animals reaches the oasis, splashing into it majestically.

I look to my right and see Dawn sitting next to me. She's wearing the same blue dress she wore on our date. She smiles and puts her hand on mine. It's warm and soft. I turn to my left and look out the window. We're underwater now, though I can still hear the plane's propeller. Whales and dolphins pass. A mermaid swims up to the window. Thick blonde hair swirls around her smiling face and naked torso. She waves, and plants a kiss on the glass, leaving an imprint of her lips before she swims away.

Dawn's hand is no longer on mine. I turn back to look at her, but she's not there. Loneliness washes over me. I turn around in my seat to see where she's gone. When I turn back, my brother Bill is sitting next to me. He's wearing a leather jacket, jeans, and a t-shirt. He looks the same as he did the last day I saw him alive. He lights a cigarette and nods.

"How you doing, Jess'?" he asks.

"I'm scared," I say.

"Why?" he asks as smoke escapes his mouth.

"I don't know what's going to happen next."

"Nobody does," Bill says as he takes another drag from the butt.

"What should I do?"

Bill shrugs. "Enjoy the ride."

I wake. Through my window's shade, I can tell the sun is now completely up. From the stereo comes a man's voice. He's speaking in a very serious tone in another language. I reach over and turn off the receiver. I roll out of bed and walk into the bathroom and pee. As I flush and wash my hands, I stare at the toilet and think about the revolver Frank left in the diner bathroom and wonder who will find it.

The kitchen's linoleum floor is cold on the bottom of my feet. Ben is sitting at the table, a steaming mug of coffee in front of him and a cigarette between his fingers. He's wearing a white t-shirt and appears to have just woken up.

"Hey," he says. "I made coffee."

"Thanks," I say, walking to the cabinet and taking out a clean mug. I pour myself a cup and add sugar and half and half. I sit down. Ben slides his cigarettes and lighter across the table. "Thanks again," I say, taking a cigarette from the pack and lighting it.

"Late night?" he asks.

I nod. "You?"

Ben nods. "Not as late as you, man. I was sound asleep when I heard you come in."

"Sorry about that."

"Nah, no need to apologize. I've got nowhere to be," he says. "How'd it go with the girl?"

"It went well," I say, nodding.

"Yeah?"

"We had a great night."

144

"That's awesome, man," Ben says before taking a sip of coffee.

I take a drag off the butt and flick the ash into the ashtray in the middle of the table, nodding.

"When you gonna see her again?"

"Um," I say, running a hand through my hair. I shake my head and smile. "I have no idea."

Ben stands and walks over to the counter as he downs the last of his coffee. He puts his mug in the sink. "Well don't wait too long, man," he says before disappearing down the hall. I hear a door shut and the sound of water in the shower being turned on.

I reach into my back pocket and take out the card with Dawn's number on it. I pick up the phone, start to dial, and then stop, holding down the disconnect button. I stare at the phone as I take another swig of coffee and one last drag off the cigarette before extinguishing it in the ashtray. I take my finger off the button and redial her number. I hold the phone up to my ear and sit back in the chair. After two rings, she picks up.

"Hello?"

"Hey," I say.

"Hey," Dawn says. I can hear a smile in her voice, it makes me smile.

"How are you?" I ask.

"I'm okay," she says. "I guess you got home."

"Yeah."

"What's up?"

"I was thinking about you," I say.

"You were?"

"I was."

"What were you thinking about me?"

"I was just remembering how much fun I had with you the other night," I say.

"Yeah?"

"Yeah." There's a long, awkward pause between us. "I was a mess when you left," I finally admit.

"It was a long, lonely drive home," she says. "I haven't stopped thinking about you since I walked out of our room."

"Really?" I ask.

"Yes," she says.

"So, how can we fix this?"

"I think we need to be together," she says.

"Can I come see you?"

"Yeah, I'm off today. Why don't you come over? I'll make us that macaroni and cheese with the breadcrumbs we'd talked about…and then maybe we can have some fun?" she says, and I can tell by the inflection in her voice that she's smiling again.

"Okay," I say.

Dawn gives me directions to her house, and I write them down on a small piece of paper I find on the counter. After we say goodbye, I eat a piece of toast with butter, then I shower and dress. The phone rings while I'm brushing my teeth. I turn off the water, replace my toothbrush in the holder, and walk into the kitchen, picking up the receiver.

"Jesse?"

"Mom."

"I just wanted to make sure you got home okay," she says.

"Oh, thanks. Yeah, I got home okay. Everything's all right. Hey, mom, I'm heading out of town for the afternoon. Is there anything you need before I split?"

"No," she says. "Where are you going?"

"I'm going to see a friend," I say.

"A lady friend?" she asks.

"Yes, mom," I say, laughing. "I'm going to see a lady friend."

"Oh! Well, that's wonderful. Is it the same lady friend you visited while you were out of town on work?"

"Yes, mom. It's the same friend."

"Well, don't let me keep you. I'll talk to you later. I love you, son."

"I love you, mom."

I hang up and walk back into my bedroom. I grab my wallet and keys and take my helmet from off the top of the refrigerator. I lock the front door and walk outside. Kids are playing, riding their bikes up and down the sidewalk, some are jumping rope, others are drawing with chalk.

I put my helmet on, get on my bike, and start it up. I drive out of the cul-de-sac, down the street, and onto the highway.

It takes me just under an hour to get to Dawn's place. She lives on one side of a duplex. Her house is similar in size and style to the one Ben and I rent.

I take off my helmet and look around. "Hey!" I hear someone yell. I look up to see Dawn smiling, leaning out of an open window. The wind plays with her hair. She looks beautiful.

"Hey!" I yell back.

"I want a ride!" she says.

"Well come down here!" I say.

The window closes. A moment later, Dawn's walking out the front door, wearing a plaid long-sleeve shirt tucked into tight faded jeans with white sneakers. She's carrying a motorcycle helmet.

"Hello," she says as she walks over, smiling brightly.

"Hello," I say.

She puts her arms around my neck. We kiss.

"You ever ride on one of these before?" I ask, looking down at the helmet in her hand.

"Once or twice," she says as she motions with her head toward a motorcycle parked on the side of the house.

"Are you fucking kidding me?"

She laughs.

"I had no idea," I say.

"I had no idea *you* rode," she says. "Let's get out of here."

I start my bike up. Dawn gets on the back. I ride slowly down the street and out onto the main road. As we're riding, I think about the people I love and the people I've lost. I think about Frank and imagine him reunited with his sister. It makes me smile.

Dawn holds me tightly around the waist. I look back at her, and even though I can't see her lips, I can tell by the sun's light illuminating her eyes through the helmet's visor that she's smiling. Maybe that yellow son of a bitch in the sky isn't so bad after all.

Acknowledgements

Thank you, Julianne Mascola, for being a constant source of support and assistance in the editing of all my novels. Thank you, Ben Hillman, for being instrumental (no pun intended) in providing suggestions regarding the jazz trio featured in this story. The Ben character is a tribute in name alone. The synopsis that appears on the back cover and online was finalized using suggestions from Gerry Pasko and Ray Mascola. Finally, thank YOU for reading my books. Your appreciation makes it all worthwhile.

Made in United States
North Haven, CT
04 January 2022

14159373R00085